BIGFOOT
THE SUMATRA ENCOUNTER

GAYNE C. YOUNG

SEVERED PRESS
HOBART TASMANIA

BIGFOOT: THE SUMATRA ENCOUNTER

ISBN: 978-1-922861-94-8

SUMATRA 1936

Arif's spine severed at impact against the tree.

His now-paralyzed body fell to the jungle floor in a twisted heap of odd angles and anomalous bends. His left arm was pinned under him, his right twisted sideways and over his head, and his legs bent out of alignment and over one another like broken scissor blades. His brain went into overtime in an effort to process what had happened to him.

And why he was unable to move.

He stared across the jungle floor in panic and disbelief. The sideways world before him was a mass of matted foliage, fallen limbs, and crawling insects. He heard the cries of his friends Abyasa and Mentawei then the angry breathing of the creature that had swung his body into the tree as if it had weighed nothing.

Arif heard the creature walk toward him then saw one of its black, leathery feet step in front of his face. The ground suddenly spun away from him and he realized that the animal had jerked him upward by his arm. Arif heard his shoulder dislocate and thought to scream but felt no pain.

Only fear.

This feeling grew and festered within him at the sight of the beast before him.

The creature that held Arif high above the ground and at arm's length stood almost eight feet tall and weighed more than 850 pounds. Its long, thick hair was the color of burnt rust, was matted with torn leaves, twigs, other jungle debris, and swarming swarmed with gnats and black flies. The stench that permeated from its hide was putrid, reminiscent of spoiled milk and musk, and it burned Arif's nostrils. The beast's canine teeth were long, yellow, and embedded with food and rot. But it was the eyes that most frightened Arif. The creature stared at him with greenish-brown eyes that mirrored rage.

Unrelenting determination.

And a sense of understanding.

Arif heard Abyasa and Mentawei call his name in terrified abandon once more then felt the anger of the beast's breath as it answered the human cries with a deafening roar. It tossed Arif aside and he came to land on the earth with a deafening thud. He heard his body hit the ground and the sound of his breath escape his body. He wept at the realization that he was moments from death and watched as his friends ran into the jungle. He saw the creature drop to all fours and rampage into the jungle tapestry after the two men.

The sight grew darker.

And darker.

Then gave way to a black void.

2.

Jack Taylor entered the small bar and paused in the doorway to allow his eyes to adjust to the dim light. He made note of where the bartender stood in relation to the bar and counted the customers that stood or sat facing the bar or any of the few tables. His eyes trained on the far corner table to see Abyasa sitting with his back against the wall as if waiting for someone to approach him or fearing that someone would come at him from behind.

Abyasa was flanked by two large men and they turned in their chairs to face Taylor in response to some unseen movement on their friend's part. Taylor walked across the rough-hewn floor, stained with spilled beer and blood from fights long past fought, warped from age and heavy humidity, to before Abyasa's table. Taylor dropped his hands onto the table and stared across it and into Abyasa's eyes.

"Twelve tiger skins."

"I no have, Taylor," Abyasa answered in broken English. "They gone."

"Cut the shit, Abby," Taylor commanded.

"It no shit," Abyasa promised. "It true. And no call me Abby! I tell you every day not call me that!"

The man seated to Abyasa's right grinded his cigarette into the center of the table and stood in a show of strength and loyalty. Taylor was surprised to see how big the man was. At six feet tall, he was just two inches shy of Taylor's height and the extra weight he carried looked concentrated in the man's chest, neck, and arms.

"No call him Abby!" the brute Indonesian demanded with one poke of his finger into Taylor's chest for every word he spoke. "You be rude white boy!"

In one swift, lightning-fast move, Taylor took the man's right finger into his hand and broke it then smashed his head downward and into the table. Blood gushed from the man's nose and mixed with his involuntary tears into a quickly spreading pool upon the table.

"Don't call me white boy," Taylor insisted.

The man to Abyasa's left flung the table upward and over in Taylor's direction. Taylor jumped backward and those in the bar crowded around Taylor and the table in a semi-circle formation to better see the excitement. Abyasa's friend came to stand in a blur of motion. He spun around in a frenzied motion that ended with a kick to Taylor's chest. Taylor was knocked backward to the ground. He launched himself upward with his Colt M1911 pistol in hand. He lunged forward and pressed the gun to his attacker's forehead.

"Abby, tell your friend here to have a seat," Taylor calmly instructed, "or you'll be wearing the back of his head on your face."

Abyasa cursed then instructed his friend to return to his seat. The man reluctantly did so and Taylor moved past him to just before Abyasa.

"Twelve tiger skins," Taylor began again. He leveled his pistol to between Abyasa's eyes. "You took them. I want them back."

"No need for gun," Abyasa calmly retorted. "Fadhlan is brother-in-law. He just helping kind of guy."

"Well, I don't like the way he helps," Taylor exclaimed, thinking of the pain in his chest. "And, what? Am I doing a family tree here? I couldn't give a shit about him. Or you. I just want my skins."

Abyasa leaned forward in his chair, closer to Taylor and his pistol.

"I tell you. I no have."

"Then give me the money you sold them for," Taylor demanded.

"I no sell," Abyasa promised.

"You stole them. What'd you do with them? Decorate your home?"

"Yes. I steal. I very sorry. But we attacked. Left skins."

"Attacked by who?" Taylor asked, getting more and more annoyed by the second.

"I no know. It not a who. It…something else," Abyasa admitted. "It like…like giant orangutan."

The crowd of revelers behind Taylor chuckled. Some called names and others shook their head in disbelief at the man with the gun to his head's admission.

"A giant orangutan took my skins?" Taylor smirked. "Is that what you're telling me, Abby?"

Abyasa spit through gritted teeth, "Don't call me Abby!"

Taylor grinned at the man's frustration then felt his face involuntary drop at the sound of a pistol being cocked next to his temple. He felt the metal barrel against his razor-shorn hair and his body clenched in anticipation of what was to come.

"Lima wants to see you," a man with a heavy Indonesian accent explained from behind the pistol.

"He can make an appointment," Taylor countered. "I'm kinda busy at the moment."

Some in the crowd that understood English laughed at Taylor's cockiness.

"You know Lima doesn't wait," the pistol bearer replied. "And neither do I. Please, don't test my patience, Mr. Taylor."

"Well, since ya said please."

Taylor knew very well about Lima's temperament. The man hadn't risen to the top by being patient.

Or by being understanding.

Taylor thought on his options for a second then tried his luck.

"Then my friend Abby here goes with us," Taylor asked. "'Cuz we've got some unfinished business."

"That is acceptable," the voice behind the pistol replied.

"I hate you, Jack Taylor," Abyasa exclaimed. "And no call me Abby!"

3.

Gajah Banua Lima fashioned himself a warlord.

He wasn't one.

He was the head of a criminal organization.

One that he took over by killing his father some twenty years earlier.

Lima and his group dealt in anything and everything that could make money.

They manufactured drugs.

They sold drugs.

They ran alcohol, participated in illegal logging, handled bets, managed prostitution, extorted businesses, murdered for hire, kidnapped, and a host of other criminal activities. In short, if it was illegal and profitable, Lima's clan not only participated in it but ruled over it.

Lima ran his criminal empire from his palatial estate on the outside of the city of Acek at the base of the Barisan Mountains. The property included a main house where his wife and children lived, a small home for his first mistress, a cottage for his second mistress, bunk houses for some of his men, and barns and farmhouses in which the people lived that tended to his palm oil planation and animals.

Lima conducted most of his business in a large, open-air longhouse built in the Dayak style with an ironwood structure and simple plank floor. He was reclined on an overstuffed couch in the center of this structure smoking hash from a hookah when his men brought Taylor before him.

"Jack Taylor, my dear old friend." Lima chuckled on a cloud of hashish. "I'm so glad you could come."

"I wasn't given a choice," Taylor chided as he took note of the armed men in the room. He counted five with rifles or shotguns standing to the side of Lima's couch, two armed with Bergmann MP35 submachines gun standing off to the side, and one standing behind a small bar in the corner of the longhouse. Although he couldn't see a firearm in the bartender's possession, he was sure he had at least a pistol if not something heavier hidden behind the bar and out of sight. These eight men, combined with the five that dragged him and Abyasa from the bar to the estate, meant there were at least 13 ways he could die if he made a move to leave before being dismissed.

"And I see you brought a friend," Lima continued. He raised his head to the five men that stood behind Taylor and added, "I don't remember sending for Abyasa. Or did I forget doing such?"

Taylor answered for his captors.

"I insisted he come," Taylor announced. "He and I have some unfinished business to discuss, and I'd hate for him to leave my sight before we conclude the matter."

Abyasa gritted his teeth in anger at his predicament.

"Very well," Lima said. "Perhaps he can help you…"

"Help me with what?" Taylor inquired before better accepting his predicament. "Cuz, ya know, you could at least offer me a drink if you're about to ask me a favor."

Lima shot Taylor a harsh look then burst into laughter. His men followed suit as did Abyasa, whose boisterous laugh revealed a mouth free from ever experiencing any dental care whatsoever.

"Always the smartass, my Taylor," Lima offered with a smile before gesturing to the man behind the bar. The man nodded and poured a tall glass of Arak Bali then delivered the distilled from palm flowers alcohol to Taylor who downed half of it in one slug.

"Good shit," Taylor complimented. "Now, what ya got?"

Lima took a long drag on his hookah then rolled his nearly 300-pound girth onto his hip.

"You traveled into my territory without paying the toll," Lima decreed to Taylor.

"It's not your territory," Taylor quickly countered.

"Yes, my friend…"

"You've never stepped foot in the upper mountains," Taylor explained. "You have no idea what's up there. The midrange is controlled by bandits that have never heard your name…"

"Still mine," Lima declared. "And you hunted it without so much as even asking."

Taylor killed the remainder of his drink in one heavy gulp then tipped his glass to the bartender who nodded in return. The man brought the bottle to Taylor and moved to pour but Taylor took the bottle and gave the barkeep the empty glass in return. Taylor took a long pull on the bottle then asked, "Where's this going?"

Lima smiled at the arrogance before him. He liked Taylor. Liked his resolve, his experience, and his acceptance of his place in the pecking order. Taylor was good in a fight, efficient with a gun, and always got the job done. His only problem was that he always had to be directed, pushed in the right direction.

"You traveled in my territory," Lima began again. "But I have a way for you to make things right."

Taylor sighed and dropped his head.

"An archeologist. An American," Lima continued, "rightly sought my permission to enter the mountains. He paid for his passage. He and his group were to be gone six weeks. They've been gone for more than ten."

"So…" Taylor countered, bringing his head out of its downward slump.

"He and his crew found something. Something valuable…"

"They're probably dead," Taylor declared. "If they made it past the bandits. If. The upper mountains are inhospitable. God damn primordial. There's a million different ways to be killed up there."

"No. They're alive and they found something," Lima decreed. "I can feel it. I know it."

"That your gut telling you that or the hash you smoke all day?" Taylor chided.

Anger flashed over Lima's round face. His men tightened their stances in response.

"Find the professor. I want what he's found," Lima bellowed. "Somebody will either pay for it or pay for him. Do this and your debt and your insult to me will be voided."

Taylor saw no way out of his situation. If he didn't go in search of the probably dead American, Lima would know and have him killed. If Taylor skipped town, Lima's people would know and have him killed. Taylor's only hope was to either find the professor alive or to find whatever he found in the mountains.

If he found anything at all, that is.

Taylor thought for a second more, took another long pull on the bottle of Arak Bali, then spoke.

"I'll find whatever I can find," Taylor explained. "But ask that you send Abby here with me. Again, we've got some unfished business that demands he stay in my presence."

Abyasa turned in shock to Taylor. He spat, "You son of the bitch!"

Lima smiled and decreed, "Abyasa will accompany you until you return."

"Thank you," Taylor said, smirking.

Abyasa scowled at Taylor and at his situation.

4.

Robert Kreipe made his way through camp and past the laborers packing crates marked, "Houston Museum and Scientific Society, Inc" to Professor Curtis Devonshire, who stood before the remains of the stone temple partially hidden by jungle foliage and the passage of time. The professor stood transfixed by the work the Indonesian diggers were doing. Despite this being their first time at an archeological dig, the men had performed beautifully, taking pride in their work and discovering the remains or partial remains of at least 25 artifacts. The finds, not including the temple itself, had included spears and spear tips, knives, beads, shields, pottery, and sculptures depicting local animals and those found only in dreams.

Or nightmares.

Animals that more resembled monstrosities of myth and pagan idolatry than those found in the real world.

But the time to decipher such mysteries was later, when the pieces were back in Houston. Now was the time for discovering and packing, as the team's days in the field were already well past their allotted time.

"Robert!" Curtis declared with great joy. "Look at them. Look at them all uncovering the mysteries of history. Discovering what civilized man has never gazed upon."

Robert smiled at the professor's enthusiasm. He took a moment to let the man enjoy what he was witnessing then returned to the thoughts that brought him to the professor in the first place.

"Professor," Robert began. "I'm afraid it's time to leave."

"Lunch already," Curtis replied without taking his gaze off the half dozen men working before him.

"No, sir," Robert explained. "Time to leave camp."

Robert had barely finished the sentence before Curtis turned to face him. He wore a look of shock and disbelief.

"Leave?! But we've only scratched the surface. Literally."

Robert nodded in understanding then continued. "We were to be here less than six weeks. We've made incredible progress but are nearly out of supplies. Out of food…"

"Andrew's out hunting now," Curtis reminded. "He always brings back something."

Robert continued nodding. "We hired these men for a set time. They want to return home. To see their families. They're growing angry. Resentful. Fresh meat won't quell that."

Curtis stared at the broken shards of the ancient structure that jutted from the jungle floor and to the men carving into the earth around them in search of clues to some past world. Leaving now would bring an end to such discoveries and all but close the book on that period.

"This will all be lost if we leave now," Curtis explained, waving his hands before him. "Lost. These men will return home and news of our discovery will spread like wildfire. Grave robbers will come. The site will be looted, and all will be lost. I've seen it happen before. Many times."

"I understand, sir," Robert assured.

Curtis stood in thought.

He thought of all that had brought him to where he now stood. He looked back on all the years of study and planning it had taken to get him from Texas to the rainforests of Sumatra. Of all the false starts he'd had. How he'd waited patiently for months for correspondence, requests, and inquiries to be answered. How he traced down every ancient text, every false map, every rumor, and every piece of passing gossip. It had taken more than a decade to prove his theory correct, and now the moment was passing.

"Curtis," Robert interrupted. "We have to leave. I'm sorry. But we have to. It's past time."

Robert nodded in understanding and in agreement.

"One more day, Robert," Curtis decreed. "Give us one more day to give the place a final sweep and then we'll leave."

Robert searched for the right thing to say but in the end simply offered, "Yes, sir."

5.

Despite being born in and having lived a large portion of his life in Ireland, Andrew Matthes had adapted well to his life in a far warmer climate. The heavy humidity and sweltering heat of Houston had taken some time to get used to, and he had spent several nights coping with painfully debilitating sunburns with massive quantities of booze, but he came to like the city and almost enjoy the weather. He enjoyed the time he spent with customers and the many hunting trips John Rigby & Company had allowed him. His employment at the legendary gunmaker's first United States store had allowed him to take clients hunting throughout North America, from the jungles of Southern Mexico to the frozen wastelands of the Polar Circle. And it was through these hunting connections that he had met Professor Curtis Devonshire.

They had met at the party of an oil man who had just returned from a safari in Africa where he had successfully taken all of the big five using custom Rigby guns he had procured from Andrew. The party was at the man's trophy room and saw more than 150 attendees. One of these attendees was a striking blonde that Andrew had hoped would come home with him but had introduced him to her much older husband Curtis instead. Oblivious that Andrew had only moments earlier made a move to bed his wife, Curtis took great interest in Andrew and by the end of the evening had asked him to accompany him to Sumatra the year following. Andrew relished the idea of embarking on the expedition and for the opportunity to take game most hunters never even got the opportunity to see.

In his almost 10 weeks in-country, he had taken a magnificent rhino of over 1,600 pounds that sported a front horn measuring an unheard of 30 inches, several sambar deer, several species of gibbon, and an absolutely gorgeous clouded leopard. Additionally, he had kept the men of the camp in good spirits with meat from mouse deer, boar, and a number of fowl species. He was on the trail of anything for the men to eat when his assigned tracker and skinner Soleh pointed to fresh tracks in the thick rot that was the jungle floor.

Andrew studied the large, three-toed impression that resembled a dinosaur track then whispered, "What the hell is that?"

Soleh thought for a moment then whispered in his very broken English, "How to say? No boar…"

"Like a boar?" Andrew questioned.

"Boar with…"

Soleh put his hand to his nose then made a wiggling motion.

Andrew watched the gesture then smiled at the pantomime and asked, "Tapir?"

Soleh looked puzzled.

"It has a trunk-like nose? Like an elephant?" Andrew questioned as he repeated Soleh's hand gesture over his own nose.

Soleh smiled and nodded then asked, "How you say?"

"Tapir," Andrew slowly enunciated. "Tapir."

Soleh nodded then pointed to the thick vale before them and led Andrew into it.

They slowly followed the tracks through the tangled tapestry of the lower rainforest. They kept to the narrow game trail and climbed over and around fallen limbs and tangled roots, past ferns the color of emeralds and still soaking wet from the early morning rains, and through puddles swarming with the larva of a dozen different insects. They stopped every few feet so Soleh could assess the tracks they followed and any other sign left in the wake of the huge mammal. They continued their cautious dance through the steam cloud that was the lower forest until they came to a wide funnel that opened to a small clearing of calf-deep grass and knee-high ferns. Soleh pointed to a distant white object that shone in a narrow beam of light, piercing the seemingly impenetrable canopy above.

Andrew and Soleh got into a crouch and eased behind a large tree that stood strangled by vines and trailed in ants. Andrew unslung his .275 Rigby from his shoulder and leaned into it, using the side of the tree as a rest. He watched the white object meander through the tall ferns. It passed behind taller plants then appeared again only to be shadowed by the darkness. Andrew stared down the open sights of his rifle in wait, following the object until the white part became whole.

Andrew estimated the tapir stood perhaps three feet at the shoulder and weighed just under 400 pounds. It was charcoal black save for its white hindquarters, had a soft pink underbelly, and was completely oblivious to being hunted. Andrew drew a bead just above the animal's front shoulder, exhaled slowly, then squeezed the trigger.

The rifle thundered.

The animal collapsed.

The clap echoed through the forest.

Andrew jacked another round into the rifle, pushed the safety on, and picked his spent shell from the jungle floor. He stood then looked to a smiling Soleh and shook his hand.

"Thank you, sir," Andrew offered.

"Much nice," Soleh replied. "It much nice."

"They taste good?"

"Taste very good. Make very good meal."

Soleh led Andrew across the opening to the downed animal. Andrew marveled at the creature, at its size, coloring, and its short, prehensile-nose trunk. He had seen a tapir in Mexico once while hunting the rainforest of Campeche but had never gotten the chance to pull the trigger. The animal before him more than made up for that disappointment.

Soleh pulled the knife from his belt and gestured with it toward the downed tapir.

"To gut?"

Andrew nodded then stepped back to allow Soleh more room to perform his duty. He fished a cigarette from the pack in his front shirt pocket, lit it, then tossed the spent match into the jungle.

Something in the direction that he flicked the match caught his eye.

Some slight movement upon the bark of a large tree.

He took two steps forward then paused. He studied the tree some five yards before him then saw a flicker of vivid blue. It was a lizard. Andrew walked slowly toward the tree, moving cautiously in an attempt to not frighten the small reptile. He got within three feet of the tree before the lizard skitted upward and out of view.

Andrew finished his cigarette, dropped it to the ground, and dug it into the earth with his boot. He raised his head then saw something in the bark of the tree where the lizard had been. He reached out and took what he quickly realized were hairs into his hand.

There were five rust-colored strands, each measuring over four inches in length. They were oily and smelled of musk. Andrew circled the tree looking for more hairs but found none. He investigated the area behind the tree and further into the jungle, and found three prints in the littered debris of the jungle floor.

"Soleh," Andrew called out into the clearing. "Come have a look."

Soleh stood from his gutting job, wiped his bloody hands on his pants, and ran to before Andrew.

"Yes, boss," Soleh asked.

Andrew held out the hairs and Soleh took them into his hand.

"What are these?" Andrew asked.

Soleh studied the hairs then smelled them.

"Look like the orangutan," Soleh theorized. "Maybe orangutan."

Andrew stepped a few feet from the tree and knelt. He pointed to the enormous tracks and asked Soleh, "These?"

Soleh kneeled and stared at the track before him in amazement. The print was more than three to four times the size of his hand and more than an inch deep. It looked like a footprint yet had an offset toe that more resembled a thumb.

"I never to see," Soleh explained. "I no know what it be."

Andrew pointed to the hairs Soleh still held in his hand. "From orangutan? These tracks from the same thing as the hairs?"

Soleh stood and shook his head.

"No orangutan track. Orangutan no that big."

Andrew nodded and returned his gaze to the tracks.

Whatever made the impressions was huge.

6.

Curtis, Robert, and Andrew completed their meal and walked from beneath the dining fly to under the stars. Their camp was located in a small clearing upon the banks of a wide river and consisted of three private tents and a dining fly for their use, a kitchen tent used by their assigned cook, and a fly which kept camp's crated supplies and the finds they would be taking with them back to Houston. The expedition's laborers slept on the ground near a fire that they used to cook, keep warm, and socialize around. There was a fire outside the kitchen tent where the cook prepared meals and a private fire for the expedition leaders nestled between their three tents.

The cook followed the three men into the night with a wooden tray holding cigars, a cutter, and lighter. Curtis, Robert, and Andrew each took a cigar, cut it, and lit up.

"Brandy, sirs?" the cook asked.

Curtis nodded in the affirmative. The cook nodded in response then backed away and turned to make his way to the kitchen tent for three sifters.

"Good man, that Agung," Curtis offered. "I'll miss him. Has done a damn fine job."

"Yeah. Good guy. I still can't pronounce his name though," Andrew said on an exhale of cigar smoke.

"Not sure that you ever really tried to pronounce his name," Curtis replied.

"Why would I, when he answers to 'Cook' and 'Hey' every time I call them in his direction?" Andrew laughed. "He can cook a mean tapir steak though. I'll give him that."

"Yes, that was much better than I thought it'd be," Robert offered.

"What'd you think it'd be?" Andrew inquired.

"I don't know," Robert admitted. "Less like pig, I suppose."

"I'm just glad it didn't taste like it looked," Curtis offered. "Ugly-looking thing, wasn't it?"

"I disagree completely, Curtis." Andrew smiled. "I take it as one unique animal. That's why I've got Darma and Soleh down by the river scraping his hide right now. Going to have him full-body mounted and placed right there in the store for all to admire."

"I always knew there was a reason you weren't married," Curtis joked. "I just didn't know the reason was your taste in décor."

The men laughed then paused their conversation when Agung returned with a tray of drinks. They took their drinks and offered thanks to Agung then watched as he returned to the kitchen tent. They made their way back toward the dining fly, pulled their chairs out to under the stars, and took a seat. They commented on how nice the weather was for their last night in camp, and on the clarity of the sky and the brightness of the stars.

Andrew detailed how he and Darma and Soleh would leave earlier than the rest of the expedition in order to hunt and to find a suitable camp for the group's first night back on the trail. Roger explained that the camp was taking back more than they had brought with them thanks to their discoveries but that the men and donkeys could easily handle the extra load. He added that because of the increased load, it would probably take them longer to return to the city of Acek. Curtis agreed with both Andrew and Roger then explained how disappointed he was that what he had discovered was fated to be looted and destroyed by those that would come after him. Roger tried his best to assuage the professor's dismal outlook but gave up after several attempts and instead changed the subject.

"I tell you what I won't miss," Roger began anew. "I will not miss the bugs."

"Agree with you on that one, Rog," Andrew exclaimed. "I've lost probably three pints of blood to the mosquitoes alone."

"It's their noise that bother me most," Curtis declared. "The constant buzzing and whining at night; it's a wonder any of us ever get any sleep."

The professor's words struck a realization in Andrew. He shot out of his chair, letting his brandy fall to the ground in the process. Both Curtis and Roger commented on Andrew's sudden movement but were silenced by the look of heavy concern on his face.

Andrew listened intently to the complete lack of sound.

The jungle was silent.

Dead silent.

Andrew reached for the Colt revolver at his hip.

But it was too late.

The darkness of the jungle blurred, giving way to a juggernaut of incredible proportions. The creature unleashed a deafening roar andthundered forward into the starlit opening. It barreled into the three men, knocking them to the ground in a blur of violence. Andrew rolled and came up with his Colt. He fired in haste and the shot creased the beast's arm. The creature grasped Andrew in its massive hand and tossed him aside into the darkness. Curtis howled in pain and rolled on the ground while clutching his chest. The creature gazed at the whimpering man in anger and brought its fist down with a heavy blow that collapsed Curtis' chest and flattened him into the earth.

Robert scrambled forward in escape. The creature took the fleeing man's head in its hand and crushed it with such pressure that the exploding pop of the skull was heard at the laborers' fire some ten yards away. The beast threw Robert's lifeless body to the side and into one of the dining fly support poles. The pole snapped and the lit gas lantern that hung upon it fell to the sisal rug, bursting into flames. The fire raced across the dry, woven mat and up the tablecloth that still lay upon the table where the men had just eaten. The flames licked the canvas fly above and ignited the entire structure.

The creature turned toward the raging inferno, roared, and beat its chest with closed fists, producing a sound of thunder.

7.

Agung was prepping the dishes from dinner to be washed when he heard the roar. Curiosity trumped his unease and he exited the kitchen tent to see what had unleashed such a frightening sound. He had just stepped out from beneath the canopy when the beast drove into Curtis, Robert, and Andrew. The animal was immense in stature, standing over eight feet tall and weighing more than 900 pounds.

Andrew's pistol fired and the outward flame revealed the creature's pelage as rusted orange and its massive canine teeth as soured-yellow in color. The beast howled at the gunshot then reached down and took the hunter in its hand. It threw Andrew aside then brought its fist down on Curtis, killing him with one blow. Agung kept his scream at bay with his hand then watched in horror as the red giant smashed Robert's skull like an egg. The beast threw Robert's lower body into the dining fly, somehow unleashing a torrent of fire.

Agung ran forward to fight the fire.

The creature spotted him and charged toward him.

Agung turned and ran toward the assumed safety of the number of laborers.

The creature's leg snagged one of the dining fly ropes. The fire-engulfed canvas was snapped free and flung forward. The flaming canvas came to land on the kitchen tent and soon engulfed the large enclosure and its contents into a storm of flame and heavy smoke.

Agung ran from the fire and the beast whose rage started it to the surviving members of the camp. The laborers were standing in confusion around the roaring fire, trying to make sense of the happenings on the other side of camp. They saw Agung running toward them and then caught sight of the creature in pursuit. The beast swatted Agung and the powerful hit sent him flying into the storm of escaping men. The beast launched forward into the men and unleashed a tempest of violence and pain. Men's chests were caved inward, limbs were dislocated or ripped from bodies, and skulls were crushed. Men screamed in fright, howled in pain, cursed their luck, and cried for quick release from unbearable pain. Bodies that landed in the fire melted in coals and filled the camp with the stench of singed hair and cooking flesh.

The beast surveyed the carnage and roared in triumph.

8.

Darma and Soleh had finished scraping the tapir's hide and had begun salting it when the first crocodiles appeared. The crocodilians were small, the largest of the three only a few inches longer than two feet, but aggressive enough that they'd climbed out of the river to devour the pieces of fat and gristle the men had pulled from the hide. The men paused in their salting to watch the small reptiles and marveled at how they shoveled through the tapir scraps in record time.

"Greedy little bastards," Soleh commented in his native Indonesian.

Darma nodded and smiled then scanned the dark river before him.

"Just hope their parents don't show up," Darma added.

"The biggest one I've ever seen had to measure over 12 feet," Soleh said. "A friend of my uncle shot it after it ate one of his pigs. Uncle said the croc swallowed the pig in one bite."

"How big was the pig?" Darma asked.

"What? I dunno," Soleh replied. "Why?"

"Makes a difference in the story," Darma replied. "It swallowing a piglet whole's no big deal."

"It was a pig pig," Soleh insisted. "Not a piglet."

"A pig pig?" Darma laughed. "What the hell's a pig pig?"

Soleh joined in the laughter and the two men chuckled for a time until a terrifying roar pierced the night air. The roar was followed by a gunshot then screams and calls for help and the cursing of men under duress.

Darma and Soleh rushed up the riverbank toward camp to witness half the camp on fire. They saw men scrambling for safety then caught glimpse of a red monstrosity in the firelight. The beast was killing everything within its sight, throwing men into the air or using them as clubs to bludgeon other men. Darma and Soleh thought to do something but knew there was nothing they could do to help their fellow laborers. They watched the beast howl in triumph over the dead bodies then turned and ran back toward the river. They jumped over the still-feeding juvenile crocs, dove into the ink-black water, and swam outward and away from the bank.

9.

"If I may be perfectly blunt…" Richard Allen continued. He leaned forward in his chair and placed his hands on the desk before him then paused before continuing. "The simple truth of the matter is that we advised—strongly, I might add—your husband not to folly into the upper Barisan Mountains. The area's a no man's land. Virtually unexplored and considered by even most of the locals to be inhospitable."

Grace Devonshire leaned forward in her seat.

"So, you're saying that you're not going to help me?" Grace paused then nodded to her brother Edward Wilson who sat beside her. "Us? Help us find my husband, Professor Devonshire, because he failed to heed your warning not to explore an unexplored area. Is that correct? Is that correct, Mr. Allen?"

"Yes, Mr. Allen," Edward added. "Is that what you're saying?"

Richard paused in thought. As the Director of the American Consulate in Acek, Sumatra, it was his responsibility to keep the Americans that visited the area safe and happy. Most people that ventured to Acek and its surrounding areas did remain safe and more or less happy because they were used to taking care of themselves. These people were generally petty criminals escaping life elsewhere, fortune seekers, or ex-military looking for a fresh start in a new place after the war.

But not Professor Curtis Devonshire.

He had come with grand ideas of exploration and half-thought-out ideas. He had come looking for the fortune of lost past, one that most had assured him didn't exist. Richard had warned him of the dangers of the Barisan Mountains, but the man had insisted on going anyway. Rumors were that he even paid a local gangster for permission to enter the area. And now the professor was lost and hadn't been heard from in weeks.

In all likelihood, the professor and his team were probably dead.

Unfortunately, it was Richard who would have to deal with the fallout.

And that included stepping on eggshells in dealing with his apparently distraught wife and none-the-brighter brother-in-law.

"No. No. No," Richard continued, trying to backtrack on his actual thoughts. "I didn't mean to imply such. Not at all. No, not at all."

Grace smiled. She pulled a cigarette from a silver cigarette case in her purse and leaned in toward her brother for him to light it. She nodded in thanks to her brother then returned her attention to Richard.

"I would consider it nothing less than an honor to assist you," Richard assured her. "The only problem is…"

"And now there's a problem," Grace clarified on a small puff of smoke.

"Not a problem, per se," Richard backtracked. "It's simply… It's simply that I don't have a staff of any size. It's just me and a few office workers. I don't have anyone that could assist you in your search outside of this office."

"Can you at least recommend someone to put us on my brother-in-law's trail?" Edward asked. "Doesn't have to be anyone officially associated with this office."

"Again, the Barisan Mountains are fright with dangers. There are bandits in the lowlands, tigers and leopards in the highlands, rumors of lost tribes, headhunters, cannibals…"

"Surely you can think of at least one man on this God-awful island brave enough to guide us up there after my husband and his expedition," Grace interrupted. "I even have a map of where he was heading to, for goodness' sake."

Richard thought for a moment then offered, "I might know of someone who would do it...for the right price."

"It goes without saying that we'll pay," Grace explained. She finished her cigarette then ground it into dust in an ashtray upon Richard's desk. "I assure you we'll pay quite well."

"Yes," Richard affirmed. "You'd have to with this gentleman, as I'm afraid he's all about money. Doesn't exactly represent the best of America here on the island, if you know what I mean."

"Who is this rather upstanding individual?" Grace asked. "What's his name and where do we find him?"

10.

"Two dollars!" Taylor scoffed.

"American," the buxom Indonesian prostitute countered with a stamp of her sandal on the wooden plank floor of the Crazy Gibbon bar. "Two dollar, American."

"American, huh?

"Yes. I say American."

Taylor smiled and leaned against his pool cue. He stared into the working girl's eyes and admitted over the loud music, "I gotta confess, Sally. I'm hardly worth two bucks. But if you can scrape together a quarter, I promise to give you at least a dime's worth of effort."

"You such asshole, Taylor," Sally said in broken English, laughing as she play-slapped Taylor's chest. "You always full of shit."

"You gonna play or work on getting a freebie," an angry American exclaimed from the other end of the pool table Taylor stood at.

"You're sure in a hurry to get beat again," Taylor boasted across the table.

"Ya got no move," the man explained. "It's you that's 'bout to lose."

Taylor came off his cue and surveyed his options. His thoughts were interrupted once more by Sally.

"Hurry up, Taylor. Beat this joker so you have two dollar!"

Taylor winked to the woman then returned once more to studying the table. He eased into position, drew his cue back, and drove it into the cue ball at an angle. The white ivory ball jumped over the black eight ball, rolled into the two ball, and drove it into the corner pocket. Taylor edged around the table, easily sunk the eight, and looked to his opponent for congratulations.

Taylor wasn't congratulated.

Instead, the burly American threw his cue onto the table and bellowed, "Ya cheating son of a bitch! You can't have balls jumping on the table! What kind of crap is that?"

"So...you don't want to play again?" Taylor joked.

"The only play we're about to do is me shutting that always-flapping smartass mouth of yours," the poor loser countered as he moved down the table and toward Taylor.

Sally stepped forward in-between Taylor and the angry man.

"Watch out, cowboy," Sally warned. "This Iron Jack Taylor. He box pro back in States."

"Stay outta this, whore!" the man countered.

Sally scowled in anger and slapped the man across the face with all her might.

"You no call me whore!"

The man chuckled at Sally's audacity and pushed her aside into the pool table. Some in the bar noticed and gathered around to watch what unfolded next. The man stepped before Taylor and said, "You're a cheating, drunken has been."

"You never answered," Taylor calmly retorted. "You don't want to play another round? Try to win your money back?"

"I ain't playing you and I sure as hell ain't paying ya."

The man cocked his arm and aimed for Taylor's jaw. Taylor interpreted the action and ducked to the side. The crowd yelled in appreciation then watched as the man threw another punch with his right. Taylor ducked this shot as well and came at the man with two quick shots to the body. The man clenched in pain then came forward at Taylor with an explosive uppercut. Taylor stepped back to avoid the punch then countered with a fast jab to the man's throat. The man grasped his throat and fought to breathe. He dropped to his knees with bulging eyes then collapsed forward into unconsciousness. Taylor reached down, fished a few bills from the man's pocket, and held them aloft for all to see.

"Just what he owes me," Taylor announced to the room before bemusing to himself. "Plus a little more for the trouble."

The crowd dissipated and Taylor handed some money to Sally.

Sally looked at the money then back to Taylor. "This not two dollar. This not even American. These Rupiah. These shit."

"Told ya, it's you paying me. Not the other way around," Taylor said, smirking.

Sally started to protest but Taylor shut her down with, "Go get us a bottle. We'll see what happens after a few drinks."

Sally smiled, placed the bills in her deep cleavage, and made her way toward the bar. Taylor waded through the sparse collection of native Sumatrans, ex-pats, fallen missionaries, AWOL sailors, and vagrants that filled the Crazy Gibbon to an empty table toward the front of the bar. He took a seat and lit a cigar. When the table shook slightly, he said without looking up, "That was quick."

"Jack Taylor," a female voice began. "I'm Grace Devonshire."

Taylor looked up and across the table to see an immaculately dressed woman. She was absolutely stunning with blonde hair, crystal blue eyes, and painted red lips.

"Of course, you are." Taylor smiled.

"And this is my brother Edward Wilson," Grace continued. "We have a proposition to discuss with you."

Edward stood and held out his hand. Taylor shook it without standing or taking his eyes off Grace.

"If you have a moment," Grace offered. "We don't want to take up any of your time."

"All I've got is time," Taylor admitted.

Sally walked to the table with a bottle of Arak Bali and two glasses in hand.

Taylor didn't look up.

"Our bottle!" Sally exclaimed.

Taylor took the bottle and glasses. "Grab us another glass, would ya, Sally?"

"Only one?!" Sally huffed, noticing that there were already three people at the table and that she'd make four.

"Sounds good. Thanks," Taylor said before sending Sally on her way with a slap to her butt.

Sally shot Taylor a dirty look and made her way back to the bar.

Grace saw this then returned her gaze to Taylor, "Mr. Taylor…"

"It's just Taylor," Taylor corrected. "There's no mister involved."

"Alright." Grace smiled. "We, my brother and I got your name from Richard Allen at the consulate. He said that you were perhaps the only man that could assist us."

"I doubt ol' Richey actually said anything nice about me. Especially considering that misunderstanding he had about me and his wife that one time," Taylor confessed. "But then stranger things have happened."

"Infidelities aside, he said you can help me, us, find my husband," Grace continued. "He and his team ventured into the upper Barisan Mountains."

Taylor tried not to react in any way to Grace's confession. He didn't want to let on that he knew anything about her husband, let alone that he was already tasked with finding him by another party, one that didn't pay in money but in life and death.

"They were supposed to return over four weeks ago," Grace explained.

"We've heard nothing," Edward continued.

"It's imperative that we find my husband," Grace added. "It's extremely, extremely important."

Taylor slumped partially in his chair. He rubbed his hand over his salt-and-pepper stubble then through his slicked back hair in thought.

"That area," Taylor offered without looking directly at Grace or Edward, "is about as nasty a place as God ever put on earth."

"Yes, we've heard," Grace rebutted.

"It's unexplored. Ripe with tigers. Leopards…"

"We've heard all this from Richard Allen and others," Grace countered. "We've heard it's inhospitable, swarming with bandits. Snakes. Insects. And that everything up there can kill a man…"

"That's just the point," Taylor interrupted. "Everything up there can kill a man. Will kill a man. And your husband hasn't been heard from in a month."

"Are you saying Curtis is dead?" Edward asked.

"I'm saying the chances of that are pretty likely," Taylor admitted. "I'm sorry."

"Then I need you to help us find proof of such," Grace demanded.

Sally returned empty handed and offered, "No more glasses. They out."

"No worries," Jack said, pulling Sally into his lap. "Our friends here were just leaving."

Grace shot Taylor a look of disgust and disappointment and stood. Edward followed suit.

"And by leaving," Taylor explained. "I mean the island. Sumatra's not a place for a gal like you. It's not safe at all."

11.

Darma and Soleh floated downstream, away from the camp that was now completely engulfed in flames. Neither man could swim very well and their staying afloat in an ever-growing current was a struggle for each. They thrashed in an effort to stay above the water and watched ahead of them for floating debris or a sandbar or something else that might help them escape their struggle. The sky above darkened quickly and with it came a heavy rain and echoes of thunder.

Soleh spotted a limb arched from the bank into the water and he called through the storm to Darma with the news. The two struggled through the rain and the current toward the branch. Soleh reached it first. He thrust his arms out of the water high above him, grabbed the limb, and pulled himself up, hugging it tight with one draped arm. He reached out for Darma, who floated with the current toward him, and took his hand. Soleh pulled Darma upward until he too was hugging the branch.

The branch gave way without warning and the two men collapsed back into the water. Soleh quickly grasped the portion of the branch still attached to the shore and held tight as Darma was swept further downstream.

"Darma!" Soleh called through the darkness. "Darma!"

Soleh's only answer was a heavy clap of thunder.

He pulled himself along the branch until he could set foot on the muddy shore. He stood then immediately scraped at the ants storming up his shoeless feet. He rushed into the tree line away from the river in his haste to escape the ants. Under the trees, he found some relief from the rain and he searched through the darkness for a place to rest. He found a stump and sat upon it. He listened to the rain and the thunder, and thought about what the last half hour had seen…then wept.

12.

Grace walked down the dark alley to the entrance door of what appeared to be an abandoned warehouse. She checked the address written on a crumbled piece of paper in her hand against the one painted in black next to the door and, finding them a match, pulled her hand back to knock. She brought her hand down toward the door just as it opened then jumped back in fright as the busty Indonesian woman from the bar backed out of the doorway toward her and the street beyond.

"You still owe me two dollar!" Sally yelled into the warehouse before turning to see Grace. "Oh. It you. From bar. Go in. Maybe he pay you."

Grace ignored the slight. Instead, she nodded and entered the dim building. Her eyes adjusted and she saw a small warehouse filled with sparse furnishings, including a couch and bed, open bathroom, and a number of crates both opened and closed. Upon these were skins of more than two dozen species of animal and the tusks of elephants.

"Jesus, lady. You don't give up."

Grace entered the warehouse, shut the door behind her, and made her way toward Taylor.

"Oh. Feel free," Taylor sarcastically continued. "Come on in."

Taylor adjusted his tattered silk bathrobe and tightened its waist belt. He gestured for Grace to sit on a worn, leather couch then walked to a closed crate that served as a bar. He filled two relatively clean glasses with ice from the ice bucket then poured an ample amount of Arak Bali in each. He gave one of the glasses to Grace, clinked hers with his, and sat in a tattered leather chair opposite the couch. Grace drank, made a sour face, then placed the glass on a stack of boxes before her.

"No," Taylor said.

"I haven't said a word," Grace countered. "At least hear me out."

"I did earlier. I haven't changed my mind since."

"I understand," Grace explained. "But my position is that you have nothing to lose."

"How's that exactly?" Taylor asked.

He took a cigar from the lapel pocket of his robe and placed it in his mouth. He fished in his pocket for a lighter but found none. Grace noticed Taylor's search, saw a lighter on the stack her drink sat upon, picked it up, and walked toward Taylor. She lit the lighter and held it in front of him. Taylor puffed his cigar to life and Grace killed the flame. She looked deep into Taylor's green eyes and whispered, "Just listen."

Taylor eased back in his chair and watched as Grace went back to her place on the couch.

He liked what he saw.

She was absolutely stunning.

"Name your price," Grace began. "Guide us into the mountains and regardless of what we find, that price will be paid."

"That's a tall order."

"I come from tall money."

"We'll need supplies, porters…"

"Done."

"My fee is pretty steep."

"Done."

Taylor let loose a smoke ring then took a drink and paused in reflection. Something about Grace didn't hold true. She was after something more than her husband but he'd yet to be able to put a finger on it.

"You're sure desperate to find this professor," Taylor goaded, looking for a response.

"He's my husband," Grace replied with little emotion.

"He's your husband, and yet you're here at two in the morning talking to me about it."

Grace was rattled.

It was a feeling that rarely struck her.

"I don't like what you're implying," she countered.

"I don't imply." Taylor smirked. "I observe. I'm a hunter."

"Hunt elsewhere, Mr. Taylor," Grace instructed as she reached for her drink.

"Call me Taylor," Taylor replied.

"Call me the woman that just hired you and I will."

Taylor smiled and stood. He walked to before Grace and held out his hand.

"Deal."

13.

Soleh was covered in insect bites, his legs and arms a painting of raised red whelps in the early morning dawn. He rose from the jungle floor, stiff and in pain, and scanned his surroundings for the first time in actual light.

The world before him was a tapestry of green, of heavy trees, bamboo, vines, ferns, and waist-high foliage. Insects whined and buzzed, and the river behind him flushed and boiled. The air smelled both fresh and of rot, and the temperature was already smoldering.

Soleh stretched his body in an attempt to quell the pain of sleeping on the jungle floor and started walking parallel to the river through the thick foliage. He walked around and through trees, over fallen logs ripe with moss and fungi, and beneath and around vines laced with thorns or covered in ants. He came to a fig tree and gorged on unripe fruit then continued onward, following the river in hopes that he'd find Darma or someone or something that could help him.

He walked for an over an hour then came to a large cut in the river bank that he couldn't cross or jump. He thought of climbing down into the river to skirt the problem then remembered the night before and the difficultly he'd had in the water and made the decision not to. He turned and followed the cut further and further into the jungle until he came to a tree that had fallen over the crevasse. The remains of the tree were large enough to walk across and far longer than the 15 or so feet width of the gorge.

Soleh looked over the edge of the cut in the earth and estimated its depth at maybe 20 feet. The bottom of the crevasse was littered with rock and half-decayed limbs, rotting leaves, and other jungle debris. He thought for a moment about continuing his path along the cut until it gave but his mind turned to his condition and how the figs hadn't been enough to quell his hunger and decided to attempt to cross the makeshift bridge. Hopefully, the other side would prove to hold more food. He climbed on the log and walked upon it until the edge of the cut.

The tree seemed sturdy.

It didn't creak or give, and it wasn't slippery although mostly covered in moss.

And it was wide enough that he could walk normally rather than by placing one foot in front of the other.

Soleh took another step forward and then another until he was completely over the ravine. He looked over the log and deep into the chasm then swallowed and continued onward at a gingerly pace.

A flock of small birds exploded outward from under the tree when Soleh reached the center of his makeshift bridge. He jumped backward in fright then dropped to his knees in an effort to keep his balance. He stayed in that position for a time, allowing his heart and breathing to slow, before standing up and continuing forward. He walked carefully and cautiously, watching his every step.

He gave a sigh of relief when he safely reached the other side of the crevasse. He jumped off the log onto the jungle floor and followed the cut in the opposite direction back toward the river. He made his way through ferns that grew to his waist and fallen-over logs half turned to earth by the passage of time. He ducked under and through tangles of vine that appeared to have been woven together to form a curtain of thorns. The morning air was heavy with humidity and what sky he could see through the jungle canopy was dark and ripe with rain. He caught a sudden whiff of copper and offal.

The smell increased in potency as he edged forward and closer to the riverbank.

He came to an outcropping of rocks that jutted from the earth some 15 feet in height. The rocks were jumbled as if they had collapsed from some structure long ago and were partially covered with vines and small bushes. He maneuvered up the rocks, using them as stairs until he came to the source of the smell. A boar, some 250 pounds, lie dead and mangled upon the rocks above him. Soleh looked to see what he had just climbed then decided to continue upward. He'd simply go around or over the boar when he reached the plateau.

He climbed another step.

His eyes were level with the boar.

He took another step then pulled himself upon the plateau.

A giant mass of red fur rose from behind the boar.

It turned and Soleh saw that it was the creature that had destroyed his camp the night before.

The beast dropped a leg ripped from the boar from its massive hand, spit a chunk of flesh from its maw, and roared. Its elongated canine teeth were yellowish gray and embedded with meat and hide.

Soleh felt the creature's breath blast him in the face and he answered its roar with a scream of his own. He turned and scrambled down the rocks toward the earth below. His foot caught in between two rocks and he tripped down the hill. He jumped up then registered a sharp pain in his right ankle. He ignored the sensation as best he could and ran along the cut toward the log bridge.

The beast leapt from the plateau and landed at the base of the hill. It rose from the crouched position of its landing and arched its back, beating its chest with its clenched fists and unleashing a deafening roar. It smelled the air and roared once more then dropped to all fours and bolted forward in chase.

Soleh ran as fast as he could. Each step sent sharp pains spasming up his right leg. His lungs burned. He could feel himself trembling in fear. He reached the fallen log and climbed atop it. He struggled forward at a brisk pace. The log shook and Soleh fell to his knees to keep from falling. He turned to see the red ape running across the log toward him with incredible ease. Soleh forced himself up and ran. He ran along the log at breakneck speed, adrenaline driving him forward. He felt the log shaking beneath him and knew the beast was just behind him. Soleh launched himself off the log toward the far side of the cut. He felt the air beneath him then a tightness in his ankle, and his neck snapped in response to being suddenly jerked backward.

The beast had Soleh's lower right leg in his hand. It swung him over its head then downward. Soleh's head crushed against the log. The beast jerked Soleh's lifeless body upward then swung it down into the log again and again until there was little left above the man's neck. The creature tossed what was left of Soleh into the crevasse and roared in triumph and delight.

14.

Darma awoke to the sound of horse hooves on loose rock.

He turned over off of his stomach and coughed then vomited a large amount of river water. He realized his hand was draped over a log then remembered how he had grabbed the log with Soleh the night before, how the log had broken, and how he had fallen back in the river. He had held onto the log, using it to keep afloat in the churning river until he had succumbed to exhaustion and apparently fell asleep.

Darma pulled himself to his knees then spit the horrible taste from his mouth. He stood and stretched then watched the three men on horses approach. The men were bandits, each armed with rifles and bandoliers of ammo that gleamed in the early morning sun. They rode to within ten feet of Darma then stood there, staring at him.

"He looks pathetic. Half-naked. He's got nothing to take," one of the riders said in his native Indonesian. "I say we kill him."

"Who dumped you on my river bank?" another rider asked.

The middle rider eased his horse closer.

"You know who I am?" the rider asked.

Darma studied the man's face. It was aged from the elements and from decades of smoking but held a quality that demanded respect.

"You're Pratam," Darma exclaimed. "The bandit no one can catch."

"Good answer." Pratam smiled and tossed Darma a canteen.

Darma drank feverishly.

"How did you come to find yourself on my riverbank?" Pratam asked.

He pulled a cigarette from his tattered shirt pocket and lit it then tossed the pack to Darma. Darma caught the pack, pulled the matches and a cigarette from it, and lit up one of his own. He took a deep drag then explained his situation.

He told Pratam and his men how he had been hired to help a hunter named Andrew Matthes. That this man was part of an expedition searching for evidence of some tribe lost to history. Darma told that the professor and his team had found such evidence and that they had stayed long after their departure date due in part to their excavating more and more finds.

"What were these objects?" Pratam interrupted. "Did they have any value?"

"Only to a white man," Darma explained. "They found broken things. Very old dishes and art."

"Yes, only a white man would search out and collect centuries-old trash," Pratam pondered aloud before instructing Darma to continue.

Darma told how Andrew and he had successfully hunted many animals and birds and how they found the enormous tracks and the strands of red hair caught in the bark of a tree after taking a tapir. He then told of the monster that killed everyone, how it was the color of an orangutan, but didn't resemble one body wise. How it had walked on hind legs like a man and then on all fours, running as fast if not faster than a horse.

Pratam listened intently to Darma's story and chided his men when they laughed. He asked Darma more about the giant creature. Darma told him all he knew. He told of the beast's height, weight, appearance, temperament, and how its wrath had destroyed the camp and killed all within it.

"No one survived but you?" Pratam inquired.

"I only know of me and my friend Soleh," Darma admitted.

"And where is Soleh?"

Darma told the story of his and Soleh's escape and how Soleh had gotten out of the river and how he had not. He told of the log and waking on the beach when he heard the horses' hooves on the rocks.

"So you have no one to confirm your story," Pratam said. "That is unfortunate. Because if such a creature existed, it could bring in much money."

"I give you my word that my story is true."

"He is a liar," one of the men on horseback exclaimed.

"I am not!" Darma countered. "Why would I make up such a thing?"

"Because you know we'll kill you if you have nothing to offer," the man countered. "And you have nothing to offer other than lies."

Darma opened his ratty shirt and pulled forth a small pouch that he wore on a leather cord around his neck. He pulled out a small knife then fished out the hairs from that he had taken from Andrew. He handed the coarse fibers to Pratam who took them in his hand and smelled them.

"These are from the beast that killed everyone but you and your friend?" Pratam asked.

"Yes," Darma replied. "Do you have hunting dogs?"

Pratam turned his head slightly in interest then answered, "I know a man, yes. He has some of the best. I can borrow his. He owes me many favors."

"Then we can find this monster and get your money. I will take you to the tracks we found. Your dogs can pick up his scent from there."

"And what do you ask of me, other than your life?" Pratam curiously inquired.

"Clothes, weapons, and a fair share of your profits."

"Anything else?" Pratam asked impressed with the young hunter.

"Only that I get first shot at the monster," Darma declared. "It took much from me."

Pratam held down his hand from his perch upon the horse. Darma took the hand and they shook.

"We have a deal," Pratam promised.

15.

"Must you watch this?"

Grace gave Taylor a stern look from her place upon the alteration fitting stand.

Taylor eased back into his chair, took a drink from his flask, and watched as Raj Paul cinched his measuring tape tight across Grace's bustline.

"I'm here to offer advice," Taylor stated. "It's not like I enjoy being here. Or that I'm asking what that measurement Raj is taking is."

Grace looked to where the measure tape sat upon her then shook her head at Taylor's juvenile nature.

"That stays between Mrs. Devonshire and me," Raj joked. "A guarded secret between a lady and her tailor."

Raj moved his tape downward to Grace's narrow waist.

Taylor watched.

And enjoyed the show.

Grace was devastatingly beautiful and had a phenomenal hourglass figure.

Taylor put Grace in her late twenties and perhaps 5'7" tall. Her striking blonde hair, smooth, tan completion, and blood-red lips and nails screamed femme fatale, and her firm, pouting bosom and shapely hips radiated the kind of heat that could melt even the strongest of good intentions. Taylor hadn't seen anything like her outside of a magazine.

"This will all be for shikar, I take it, Mr. Taylor?" Raj asked, moving down to Grace's hips.

"Yes," Taylor answered.

"Shikar?" Grace questioned. "Did I say that correctly? What is it?"

"Safari," Taylor answered before turning his attention back to Raj. "We'll be in the mountains several weeks. We'll need…"

Raj cut Taylor off.

"I understand, sir. She and Mr. Edwards will be more than prepared."

Raj draped the measuring tape around his neck and helped Grace down from her stand.

"Mrs. Devonshire," Raj began. "I urge you to abandon conventional fashion standards and adhere to my suggestion of trousers. I believe they're much better suited to the endeavor that lies before you."

Grace nodded then changed her mind.

"Make it half trousers, half skirts."

Raj nodded then excused himself.

"Your turn," Grace offered to Taylor.

"I have clothes," Taylor rebutted.

Grace looked Taylor up and down as he sat slouched in the chair.

He had rugged good looks and charm to match. He was tall, had a broad chest, and carried the appearance of youth despite her guessing that he was closing in on 40. He could do with a shave and a haircut but for now, clothes would have to do.

"I'll pass," Taylor said.

He stood and walked to Grace. He held out his flask and she asked, "Is it that palm flower drink again?"

"Arak Bali," Taylor replied and explained. "Yes. That's what it is."

"Is that all there is to drink in this country?"

"No." Taylor smiled. "I can put you onto some nice beers as well if you like."

"Maybe after we get you fitted," Grace compromised.

"I've got all the clothes I need for the field," Taylor explained. "But I do know a place where your money would be better served."

16.

Jim Manry was an arms dealer.

He sold guns and ammunition.

He sold them to fellow ex-pats and Sumatra locals with no questions asked.

Except Taylor.

"How you paying for this?" Jim griped.

"Why ya treat me with such disdain, Jim?" Taylor countered.

"Cuz I've dealt with you before," Jim reminded him. "That's why."

"I'm taking care of Mr. Taylor's transactions today," Grace offered. "We're going on shikar and Mr. Taylor's our professional hunter."

"I see," Jim replied.

Grace found this comment ironic odd given that Jim only had one eye. In fact, Jim appeared to be missing quite a bit. He wore a brown leather patch over his left eye, had a dollar-sized burn mark on his lower jaw, and was missing two fingers from his right hand. Grace wondered if all these injuries had occurred at once or if he had spent a lifetime obtaining them.

"And you are?" Jim asked, almost drooling at Grace's beauty.

Grace held out her hand and introduced herself.

"So, you have what I asked for or not?" Taylor said, interrupting the formalities at hand.

"Yeah, I ran it all down," Jim said with a groan. "Not sure why I did. Like I said, I've dealt with you before."

"And I've always paid you," Taylor insisted.

Jim stared at Taylor with his one good eye.

"Okay," Taylor confessed. "Not always on time. But I always paid you."

Jim ignored the excuse and instead turned to rummage through some boxes then came back up on the counter with several cartons.

"Ten boxes .375 Holland & Holland Magnum," Jim began.

"I said 15 boxes," Taylor countered.

"Yeah, well, ya get 10 'cuz that's what I got!"

"I'm sure that will be fine, Jim," Grace almost cooed, trying to calm the gun dealer's apparently perpetually pissed temperament.

Jim placed a large piece of canvas on the counter and then brought out the next item.

"Jeffery .450/400 Nitro Express."

Taylor took the double rifle and placed it to his shoulder. He looked down the barrels then rhetorically asked, "Baby, where've you been all my life?"

"Ten cartons of ammo for the double," Jim announced. "Not 15."

"Thank you, Jim," Grace continued.

Jim placed two pistols on the counter and several boxes of ammo for each. Taylor picked up one of the pistols and handed it to Grace.

"Smith & Wesson HE2. Fires .45 ACP," Taylor explained. "I got one for you and one your brother."

"Then I'm just in time," Edward exclaimed as he walked in the door.

"Who are you?" Jim barked, watching the man joyfully almost prance through the store toward him.

"He's with us, Jim," Grace explained. "He's my brother. He was finishing up at the tailor for us."

Taylor showed the pistols to Grace and Edward and explained that it fired the same ammunition as the 1911 he carried. Grace and Edward insisted that they had grown up with firearms and were quite proficient with them. Taylor said that Jim had cartridge belts and holsters for each of them and that they should start wearing the arms immediately. Taylor's lecture was interrupted by Jim putting yet another firearm on the counter.

"Thompson submachine gun and two drums. Fully   loaded."

"Let's add one more drum," Taylor requested.

"Goddamnit, Taylor! Ya get what I give ya! You come in here to buy arms or bust my goddamn chops?!"

"That's fine, Jim. Really," Grace tried.

"No, miss. It ain't!" Jim exploded. "I been dealing with Taylor's shit here for going on a decade…"

"Believe me, Jim. I understand. And I've only known him two days."

Grace gave Jim a big smile.

He halfway smiled in return.

"I'm sorry I blew up like that," Jim apologized.

"Perfectly understandable, Jim," Grace appeased. "I understand completely."

"Yeah, Jim." Taylor chuckled. "We understand. We do."

Jim raged.

"Get the hell outta' my shop, Taylor! Now! I dunno why you even need a goddamn Tommy gun. You gonna St. Valentine's Day massacre some tigers in the mountains or some shit? And yet I tracked one down for your sorry ass, you ungrateful son a' bitch!"

Taylor laughed, reached across the counter, and patted Jim on the cheek.

"Always such a good boy, Jim. No wonder I love you."

Jim lunged across the counter but was too slow. Taylor backed away laughing and said, "My lovely assistant will get the guns. And Grace will pay."

Edward frowned.

Jim boiled.

And Grace offered under her breath, "I have no idea why that man's growing on me."

17.

They headed into the jungle at dawn.

Taylor, Grace, Edward, and Abyasa each rode a horse while the nine porters and one cook walked or led donkeys carrying supplies. They followed trails long established by subsistence farmers who traveled into the lower mountains for wood or to hunt and those looking for a starting point that led into the unknown. They encountered no one for over two hours until they came upon a young boy walking in the opposite direction with a load of sticks on his back. The boy smiled at Grace as he passed but made no eye contact with the remainder of the group, passing by them and their mounts as if they weren't there at all.

The group continued onward and upward, gaining in elevation as they made their way deeper and deeper into the mountains. The trail grew narrower and more enveloped by the ever-encroaching jungle. The trail widened a bit, allowing for Grace to ride alongside Taylor, and she took the opportunity to pass the time with conversation.

"How long have you had that hat?" Grace began, referencing the tattered, wide-brimmed, almost-crushed fedora he wore atop his head.

"A lot longer than you've had yours," Taylor said, smiling.

"I only got mine a few days ago."

"Well, there you go."

"What breed of horses are these?" Edward asked from just behind Grace and Taylor.

"They're quite hardy."

"Bali," Taylor replied. "They're tough as hell. Don't require shoes."

Edward smiled at his new gained knowledge, patted his horse along the neck, then looked to Abyasa behind him and to the left.

"Great animals, aren't they?"

Abyasa rolled his eyes at his being on the expedition and fell further behind Edward so as to not have to speak to him.

"Are we making good time?" Grace asked Taylor.

"So far so good," Taylor answered. "But then we're still more or less in civilization."

Grace looked to the jungle on her left and right and above here. She found it hard to believe that the primordial green tunnel she was traveling through was anyone's definition of civilization.

The expedition continued onward, traveling further and further into the jungle and away from Acek. They stopped for a cold lunch shortly after one and took their time eating the simple meal packed by the cook. Afterward, Taylor lit a cigar and mounted his horse. He took his new Jeffery .450/400 Nitro Express from its scabbard and placed it across his lap. Grace noted this and inquired about it as she mounted her horse.

"Are you anticipating that we'll see game?" Grace inquired.

"Just being prepared," Taylor offered.

"For what?"

"Anything."

Taylor eased his horse forward and the expedition followed. Grace rode alongside him.

Taylor led the party along the trail that winded up and over a mountain then down into a valley. The expedition baked in the sun and stewed in the stiffing humidity when under the canopy. The air smelled of flowers in bloom and of rotting leaves, musk, and wood. The palate of colors carried a thousand shades of green with hundreds of browns and dozens of vibrant reds and yellows. They heard the angry call of gibbons, and the sing-song of birds. They listened to the whining of insects and the buzzing of flies.

Not used to the extreme heat, Grace and Edward became fatigued as the day wore on, and Taylor pressured them to keep drinking water. He rode alongside Grace, reached over, pulled the scarf from around her neck, and soaked it in water from his canteen. He rung the garment out and handed it back to Grace who draped it around her neck and thanked Taylor for his consideration. Edward saw this and did the same with his bandanna and canteen and found the temporary results extremely satisfying.

Taylor was used to the heat and the humidity, and had no problem with either. He spent his time in the saddle smoking his cigars, drinking from his flask, watching for trouble, and fending off questions from Grace. She had done far better this first day of the trip than he thought she would. He had halfway expected her to give up by lunch but was pleasantly surprised to find that her determination and fortitude were just as strong as her beauty. Still, there was something about her that he had yet to figure. Some underlying aspect he was sure was there but had yet to surface.

"We'll camp here for the night," Taylor both announced and instructed.

Grace looked at him and smiled.

The day had been exhausting and she was ready to see it come to an end.

18.

Taylor, Grace, and Edward had drinks while the camp was being set up.

Abyasa took on the role of camp boss and had the men set up tents, a dining fly, gather wood, build several fires, and ensure that the cook began the evening meal. Abyasa checked on the men and their progress, chastised those in need of such, and praised others when he felt it was deserved. As instructed, Abyasa set Grace's tent on the opposite side of camp, away from the tents to be occupied by Taylor and Edward. Grace saw this and insisted that her tent be placed closer to the others. She didn't explain the reason for the move, nor did anyone ask for an explanation.

"Mrs. Devonshire," Abyasa politely interrupted. "Your tent is ready."

Grace stood from the tree she was leaning upon, brushed the back of her khaki trousers, thanked Abyasa, and followed him as he led her away from where Taylor and Edward still rested.

"Thank you, Abby," Taylor called after.

Abyasa spun around with a dirty look and threatened, "No call me Abby!"

Grace entered her tent to find it more than welcoming. She had a spacious cot with a mattress draped in mosquito netting, a dressing table with a mirror and sink bowl, a chair, and a gas lantern. The trunk containing her clothing and personal items was placed upon a stand at the foot of her cot, as was a stack of towels.

"Your water ready," Abyasa offered, standing next to the break-down, four-post shower at the rear of her tent.

Grace thanked Abyasa and watched him leave. She closed the flaps of her tent, disrobed, and entered the very confining but much-deserved shower. The water was lukewarm but felt wonderful. She washed her hair and body then stood under the showerhead and let the water cascade over her until the small tank that held it ran dry. She exited the shower, dried off, then dressed for dinner. She chose one of the skirts Raj made for her over trousers and combined it with a loose-fitting white blouse.

"Where's Eddie?" Grace asked as she took a seat under the dining fly.

Taylor stood when she entered the covering then handed her a bottle of beer.

"It's not cold," Taylor explained. "But thanks to it hanging in the cooling bag, it's not warm either. Well, real warm."

The two clinked bottles then drank.

Taylor sat and said, "Oh. Your brother's cleaning up a bit before dinner. Does he go by Eddie? He introduced himself as Edward, but you just called—"

"I call him Eddie. Or Ed," Grace admitted. "Everyone else calls him Edward. He calls me Gracie."

Taylor flicked his eyebrows in understanding and agreement then lit a cigar. Grace fished a cigarette from her pocket and Taylor leaned in to light it for her. The two smoked quietly for a time then Grace broke the silence with more questions.

"Taylor. Why do people call you that rather than your first name?"

"Habit, I guess. Coaches called me by my last name in high school. They call ya by your last name in the AEF…"

"You were in the American Expeditionary Forces? Were you in the war?"

Taylor nodded and blew three smoke rings in quick succession.

"What did you do?"

"I was a pilot."

"What did you fly?"

"Whatever they told me. Sopwith Camel mostly."

"Are they the ones with two wings? You know, on top of each other?"

"Yes. It's a biplane."

Grace sensed Taylor didn't want to talk about his time in the war.

That was a common trait with most of the veterans she'd met, including her husband.

She returned to the topic of names.

"In the bar, the night we first met. Your lady friend called you Iron Jack."

"That wasn't my lady friend," Taylor scoffed.

"She wasn't?" Grace chided. "She was at your home later that night. At two in the morning, I might add."

"So were you," Taylor countered. "If I might add."

Grace lowered her head in a half smile.

"Iron Jack? That's where my confusion on who is and who is not your lady friend began."

Taylor blew another three smoke rings.

"I boxed some back in the States. They called me 'Iron Jack.'"

"Why?"

"Lots of reasons. Had an iron jaw. Iron build. Could hit like an anvil."

Grace snickered.

"And who said these things?"

"Fans. The press."

"Fans and press?" Edwards asked as he came under the fly.

He was freshly scrubbed and had his blond hair slicked back. It highlighted his freshly sunburned face.

"What are we talking about?" Edward continued.

"Nothing of any importance," Grace offered with a devious smile. "Nothing."

19.

"Here."

Darma kneeled over the tracks Andrew had asked him about what seemed a lifetime ago.

"Keep those dogs quiet!" Pratam yelled to Vikal.

Vikal gave control of two of the dogs to Intan and pulled hard on the leashes of the other two. The dogs fought and snarled then yelped when yanked backward.

Pratam walked to next to Darma and knelt.

The tracks were old but had yet to crack or fall in upon themselves.

"Looks like a man's footprint," Pratam explained.

"No man made this," Darma countered. "Look how the one toe is offset from the others."

"Like an orangutan," Pratam offered.

"That was no orangutan that attacked us."

"You said it was dark."

"The sky was bright. So was the fire," Darma insisted. "I tell you. It was something else. It was a monster."

Pratam stood.

"Show me the camp," he demanded.

Darma stood.

"No."

Pratam fumed.

"You do not get to tell me 'No.'"

"There is nothing there but death. Dead bodies."

"And the freshest tracks we know of."

Darma knew Pratam was right.

But he didn't want to admit it.

Or rather to see the corpses of the men he once knew as friends.

He thought on the matter for a moment.

Returning to camp was the best way to find the beast and finding the beast would allow him to kill it.

Allow him to take revenge for his friends.

And to make money in the process.

Darma looked at Pratam and then to the sky above.

"You're right."

"I know," Pratam insisted.

"It's getting late," Darma observed. "We should camp here tonight. We can head for the camp first thing in the morning."

Pratam agreed and yelled to his men to tether the dogs then pulled his hash pipe from his saddlebag, sat with his back against a tree, and began smoking.

"Make a fire," Pratam demanded. "Can't have a camp without a fire."

The fire was made and the men sat around it smoking hash and drinking from a shared bottle. The shared with each other stories of hunting, banditry, and life in general. They told lies about women, bragged about the children they acknowledged as their offspring, and wondered about the ones they had fathered on accident and never seen. They talked about how much money the carcass of the giant red beast would bring and what they would do with the money once they had it. They discussed all this and more before each falling asleep in the warm glow of the fire.

The men rose at dawn and ate a cold breakfast before heading out. Each man rode a horse except Vikal, who led the dogs. Darma led them through thick jungle and across a ridge that stood guard over alternating pockets of impenetrable foliage and open fields of grass. They followed the ridge for more than two hours before they saw the vultures. Some were perched just inside the jungle canopy below them or riding air currents above them.

The men continued along the ridge and then down a cut trail that led through a deep thicket and finally into camp. The scene that unfolded before the men was one of nightmares. A sounder of five boars ripped and tore at human cadavers as vultures hopped in between them in an attempt to get at freshly cut meat. Clouds of black flies swarmed over pools of dried blood and offal, fighting for purchase among the carpet of ants that laid claim to the food stuff first. There were piles of ash and debris where tents and furnishings had once been, along with still-smoldering logs scattered by violence from the fire once used to bring men together.

Darma dismounted and dry-heaved at the sight and smell. He tied his horse to a tree just outside of camp and walked through the carnage on foot. Pratam dismounted then handed the reins of his horse to Intan who dismounted and tied the two horses to the same tree, as did Darma. Vikal stayed in place with the dogs and watched as Pratam and Intan followed Darma.

"Here. Here. Here," Darma announced as he walked over the massive set of prints left by the camp's attacker.

Pratam and Intan followed in disbelief and wonder.

They reached the place where Darma last saw the beast.

"The beast was here when Soleh and I jumped into the river," Darma explained.

Darma leaned down over the tracks and ran his fingers over the huge impression left in the ground. He spotted a small clump of hairs embedded in the earth, took them into his hands, and stood.

"Get the dogs," he commanded. "We start here."

20.

Darma, Pratam, Intan, and Vikal followed the dogs for two hours, stopping only to let the animals drink or cool off. The dogs were Thai ridgebacks, bred for hunting and guarding, with massive bodies weighing 70 pounds of pure muscle apiece. All were yellow except for the lead bitch who was dark red and covered in scars from past encounters with boars. The dogs exploded into a frenzy when the hunting party reached a densely wooded hummock. The men quickly tied their horses, grabbed the firearms, and prepared to unleash the dogs.

"I get the first shot!" Darma exclaimed as he nervously checked the rusty .30-30 Winchester Pratam had provided him with.

Vikal fought for control of the dogs as they jumped and fought to be released. They barked in excitement and their cacophony was answered by a roar from within the darkened jungle before them that stood their ridged dorsal hair on end and had the men each wondering what they had spent the day pursuing. Vikal looked to Pratam for clarification after hearing the deafening roar.

"Are you sure about this?" Vikal cowered in fear.

"Release them," Pratam angrily commanded. "Send them in after it!"

Vikal did as he was told. He released the dogs and they tore forward in raged pursuit. They ran forward and disappeared into the underbrush. Their barks echoed from within the trees down to the men who fought to keep up.

Darma fought his way into the jungle. He parted through small trees standing inches apart with vines tied between them, and through ferns and bushes that grew from the ground and trunks of trees. Pratam, Intan, and Vikal fought to keep after him and their quest was made easier by Darma's vengeful determination before them. The dogs' calls changed in tune from fierce determination to animals holding their prey at bay. The men burst forth into a small clearing to see the dogs surrounding the beast they'd come in search of. All were in disbelief at the giant's size and strength.

It was a monster in every sense of the word.

It was gigantic, covered in rust-colored fur, and furious at everything it surveyed. Its maw was streaked with blood and food stuff from the object it held in its hand. Darma stared intently at the object then gasped in the realization that it was the remains of a human leg. Darma was enraged.

The dogs had the creature surrounded and each took a turn at lunging forward in an attempt to be the first to pull it to the ground.

Darma fought his fear and engaged his hatred for the creature.

He raised the rifle to his shoulder.

The creature lunged forward and took the red dog in its hand.

Darma drew a bead on the creature's head.

The beast hurled the dog at Darma.

Darma fired.

His bullet struck the dog dead center.

The dog howled and twisted in the air before hitting Darma in the chest.

Darma was knocked backward and to the ground.

The creature grabbed a dog in each hand and crushed them.

The dogs whimpered as their ribcages collapsed inward and pierced their lungs.

The beast rampaged toward Darma.

Darma fought to get to his knees.

The beast boxed Darma's head with the dead dogs.

Darma's neck snapped and he fell dead.

The beast tossed the animals to the wayside, grabbed Darma's lifeless body, and swung it like a club into the remaining dogs. Pratam raised his rifle and fired just as the man he gave a second chance to on the river's cadaver slammed into him, knocking him to the ground. The beast placed its humongous foot upon Pratam's face and drove it into the ground until the earth gave no more, his skull exploding outward, pouring forth a pool of gray and red ooze.

Intan and Vikal fired their weapons at the beast in total fear, the shaking in their arms sending each bullet wayward and far off its target. The creature howled then threw Darma's battered corpse toward them. The men dodged the body but were unable to escape the monster that drove down on them. It grabbed a man in each hand and ran them into two trees, smashing their bodies into the bark and into death. The creature pulled back the bodies then slammed them together and dropped them to the ground. The monstrosity reared back and beat its chest repeatedly in triumph.

The remaining dogs whimpered and fled into the underbrush.

21.

By their third day on the trail, the expedition had fallen into sync and worked most of the kinks out.

Grace and Edward had become accustomed to their horses, and had more or less come to tolerate the heat and humidity. Abyasa had taken to his role as camp boss and found that he was a much better manager and host than he was hunter and thief. He quickly understood what Grace and Edward desired in the way of comforts each night. Abyasa still resented Taylor and his forcing him to accompany his expedition but understood the reason he was.

They traveled through an area recovering from a flash fire started by lightning that carried fresh grasses and small shrubs but was dominated by skeletal trees that stood dead in the blazing sun. This nightmarish landscape gave way to thick jungle and they traveled upon game trails cut by sambar deer and tapir. The canopy above them blocked out the sun except for a few errant narrow beams of light that shone down to illuminate a world that would otherwise live in a state of perpetual dusk. Taylor led the way with Grace riding just to his left and behind him. She was followed by Edward, then Abyasa, and the others.

"Don't look up, Gracie," Edward taunted. "Ya won't like what you see."

Grace looked into the upper canopy to see several dozen black and brown objects hanging from limbs. At first, she thought they were some sort of fruit or gourds but realized they weren't when one stretched thin, leathery wings outward in a span measuring four feet.

"My God," she shrieked. "What…are they? Buzzards? Hanging upside down like that?"

Edward laughed.

"Bats," Taylor replied. "Flying foxes, actually."

Grace shook in disgust and partial fear.

"Are they dangerous?" she quivered in question. "Do they drink blood? Are they…vampire bats?"

Edward continued laughing.

"Shut up, Eddie," Grace countered, the tone of her delivery taking her back to childhood.

"No. They're harmless," Taylor assured Grace. "They eat fruit. Flowers. Abby says they taste good too."

"Don't call me Abby!" Abyasa demanded.

"Is that true though, Abyasa?" Grace searched for clarification. "You eat those things?"

"Yes," Abyasa asserted. "Taste good."

"He says they taste like chicken," Taylor chided.

"No, it don't!" Abyasa retorted in angry broken English. "Chicken taste like fly fox."

The colony in the trees above them suddenly dropped from their perches and spiraled into flight. Their combined wings fanned the canopy, sending leaves and debris raining down on the expedition members below.

Taylor heard something.

He pulled tight on the reins, bringing his horse to a halt then turned to face those behind him. A blur of black and charred orange shot from the forest into Edward's horse. The mount twisted and neighed in shock then fell over, taking Edward with it. Edward was pinned beneath the horse and turned in struggle just in time to see the blur jet around. It hissed in fevered anger and sprung forward. Taylor dropped from his horse, raised his Jeffery, and fired. The tiger exploded backward and spun wildly in the air. Taylor fired again and the big cat pitched and skidded into the jungle floor. The jungle was a frenzy of horse trumpets, donkeys braying, the confusion of men, and Grace vocalizing her utter shock. Taylor reloaded and rushed forward to ensure the cat was dead. Grace calmed her mount, dropped to the ground, and hurried to Edward. Taylor and Abyasa met her and together pulled Edward from under the horse.

Blood shot from the animal's neck as it struggled to rise. Taylor passed his rifle to Abyasa then drew his .45 and knelt at the side of the suffering horse. Grace started to protest then turned her head away as Taylor ceased the horse's anguish with a quick shot to the head. He returned to Edward, and he and Abyasa helped him to his feet. Edward waved them off.

"I'm... I'm fine," Edward stuttered. "Shaken but... I'm fine."

He pushed a nervous Grace away from him then relented and let her embrace him in a deep hug.

"I'm fine, sis. Promise you," Edward exclaimed.

Taylor opened his flask and handed it to Edward who took it and nearly drained it.

"Are you sure...sure you're...?" Grace stammered. "It came so fast... I... I've never..."

"Edward," Taylor commanded in a stern voice. "Look at me."

Edward did as he was instructed.

"You okay?" Taylor asked.

Edward nodded that he was and Taylor turned to Abyasa.

"Go ahead. Find the next best place to camp…"

Taylor paused in instruction to see the remainder of his team circled around the dead tiger. He made his way to the men to hear them all mumbling the same thing.

"Setan," they said. "Setan."

22.

Camp was established a half mile from the tiger attack in a small clearing that was surrounded on all sides by towering dipterocarp trees chocked with lianas vines that hung like hundred-foot snakes from the canopy. Grace and Edward both settled into their tents and each took showers that required several refills of warm water by the laborers. Taylor knew they were each rattled and gave them their time alone to deal with their shock in their own way.

Taylor and Abyasa returned to the downed tiger and skinned it. Both marveled at the massive predator's dark coloration that was unlike anything either had ever seen before. The tiger was almost completely black with only a few stripes of burnt orange.

"It no natural. Very strange," Abyasa nervously confessed.

"You're starting to sound like the others," Taylor countered.

"They think bad omen," Abyasa reported. "Some talk they leave."

"Omen?! Omen of what? Omen of the freak tiger?"

"I dunno. They just say it bad. Bad omen of things to come."

"What do you think?" Taylor asked in true interest.

Abyasa was his lifeline to the men that could make or break the expedition. Taylor needed to know if Abyasa was leading or following.

Abyasa paused before answering.

"I think tiger very ugly," Abyasa offered with a smile. "You should give to me. I get rid of it for you."

Taylor laughed.

"I bet you would," Taylor agreed. "Have no doubt of that."

Taylor and Abyasa folded the unique hide, mounted their horses, and rode the short distance back to camp. Abyasa took the horses to be tended to and Taylor went to check on his clients. He found Edward reading outside his tent and Grace taking a nap within hers. Taylor let them be and took a much-needed shower.

Grace and Edward said little at dinner other than making small talk or inquiring about the journey ahead. Taylor said that, based on the information he'd been provided with, he felt they would reach the professor's camp within two if not three more days. Grace said the sooner they could retrieve her husband and return to civilization the better. Edward said that he agreed and couldn't wait to board a plane for the long journey back to Houston.

"About my horse, the horse I was riding..." Edward said, changing the subject.

"He was put to good use," Taylor interrupted.

"Wait. What?" Edward was confused.

"He was eaten," Taylor explained.

"Eaten?!" Grace was shocked. She looked at her empty plate then to Taylor.

"No. We had beefsteak," Taylor assured her. "The men had horse."

Grace made a face of disgust and pushed her plate away from her to the center of the table.

Edward grinned and said, "I was actually asking about the horse to see if I'd be walking tomorrow. But good to know he wasn't put to waste."

Grace snickered then burst into laughter. Edward joined in, and even Taylor snickered.

The dishes were cleared and the three sat under the dining fly drinking, smoking, talking, and laughing. A sudden downpour brought sheets of rain and a sudden temperature drop. All decided to call it a night and returned to their tents. Taylor waited until Edward and Grace had retreated to theirs then made his way through the rain to his.

He unbuttoned his wet shirt then paused to pour a drink. He opened a new bottle of Arak Bali then heard his tent flap open. He turned to see Grace enter his tent.

"Pour me one of those," Grace instructed, her voice sultry and direct.

Her blonde hair was rain damp and slicked back, her lips freshly touched up, and her blouse unbuttoned lower than at dinner, clinging to her from the downpour.

Taylor nodded, opened the bottle, and took two glasses from the trunk at the end of his cot.

"The tiger...it just has me so rattled," Grace explained. "I just..."

Taylor walked across the tent, bottle and glasses in hand, toward Grace.

"I just know I won't be able to sleep. I thought maybe another drink..."

Taylor placed the bottle and the glasses on the vanity table Grace stood next to. He took Grace by the waist and pulled her to him.

Grace resisted.

"I'm married."

"Doesn't matter."

"Yes, it does."

"It doesn't or you wouldn't be here."

Taylor pulled Grace into him and kissed her.

She backed away, seductively removed her clothing, and led Taylor to his cot.

23.

Grace lit a cigarette, pulled the mosquito netting back around the bed, then rested her head on Taylor's chest. She took a drag off her cigarette then handed it to Taylor. The rain outside the tent was pounding, and the air inside the tent was cool and heavy with the smells of sex, smoke, perfume, and Arak Bali. Grace took another drag on the cigarette then passed it back to Taylor and buried her head further into Taylor's chest.

"I loved Curtis," Grace began on a faint voice. "I really did. But then he changed."

"Things always change," Taylor stated. "Life wouldn't be life otherwise."

"People said I married him for money. I didn't. I swear that to you."

Taylor adjusted the pillow behind his head and upper back then listened as Grace told the story of her marriage falling apart and how and why she came to be in Sumatra. She told of the fights, small at first, that ended with Curtis raising his voice, then yelling, then screaming. How he apologized after slapping her the first time then got to the point where hitting her was an almost daily habit. Grace had been elated when he'd decided to test his findings in Sumatra. Their time apart from one another had given her time to assess her life and to make the difficult decision to leave him. She had decided to serve him divorce papers with her brother as witness in the hopes of him never returning to America.

It would be better if he stayed is Sumatra.

Better for all involved.

"I'm not asking him for anything. He can keep his money. I just want out," Grace continued. "But I'm just scared of what he'll do when I tell him. Very scared."

"He'll do nothing," Taylor insisted. "I'll make sure of it."

Grace smiled then leaned into Taylor with a kiss.

"Taylor!" a voice boomed from the rain.

Taylor pushed Grace away from him and answered the call with a question, "What!"

"Two leave," the voice replied.

"Get in here!" Taylor barked.

Abyasa came into the tent. The rain tried to follow him, but he quickly pulled close the tent flap. He saw Grace's naked back lying next to Taylor and looked to the floor out of respect.

"Sorry bother you, Taylor. Two men leave."

"What?!" Taylor angrily retorted.

"Say tiger bad omen."

"Idiots!" Taylor barked even louder. "Goddamn idiots. What'd they take?"

"Nothing. They try to take horse. Supplies. I stop."

"Good."

"Yes."

"Good job. Thanks, Abby."

"Name is no Abby. It's Abyasa. No call me Abby."

Taylor ignored Abyasa's tirade and instead mused, "Deserted! In the middle of a goddamn thunderstorm! Great! I hope a lightning bolt goes straight up their asses!"

Grace buried her head into Taylor's chest and tried not to laugh.

24.

The storm the night before turned the trail into a quagmire of mud and jungle runoff. Wind-broken limbs, lightning-struck logs, and other debris littered the passage. The going was slow and made even more so by the absence of the two deserted laborers. Edward rode one of the reserve horses, and both he and Grace were more cautious than they had been the day before. They watched the trail before them and behind them, studying the jungle to either side and above them. Because of this, they saw more of the island than they had during the entire duration of the expedition. They spotted gibbons swinging in the trees above, flying foxes feeding among purple flowers, a mouse deer dart through the undergrowth, colorful birds and butterflies, and insects of a hundred different species.

They traveled along the trail that led through the jungle, higher and higher into the mountains for hours without taking a break. Abyasa requested to Taylor that the group take an early lunch so he could assess how the men were handling the loads left by the two deserters. Taylor agreed and said he'd stop as soon as they found a good spot to do so. He found one roughly a half hour later when Abyasa called from his horse to Taylor, "Bungai Bankai." Taylor pulled tight on the reins and looked to where Abyasa was pointing then called for the group to halt. Taylor dismounted, followed by Grace, Edward, and Abyasa.

"Want to show y'all something," Taylor informed Grace and Edward, his voice tinged with reserved excitement.

Taylor led the two off the trail into the jungle to a small opening that contained a tall plant that measured over eight feet in height. The odd-looking plant resembled lettuce rolled into a tube and was painted along the top in shades of vivid purple and soft lavender.

"What is it?" Grace asked, circling the strange shrub, careful not to touch it.

"Locals call it a Bungai Bankai. Corpse flower," Taylor explained.

"Corpse flower?" Grace repeated. "What a dreadful name."

"Why is it called such a thing?" Edward asked.

"Cuz when it opens up every few years, it smells like death," Taylor explained. "Smells like rotting flesh. It's god-awful."

"Why?" Grace asked, still circling the plant.

"They say it's to attract flies and other insects…"

"To eat them? Is it carnivorous? Like a…what are those dreaded…a flytrap? Like a Venus flytrap?" Edward interrupted.

Grace stepped away from the flower at Edward's questions.

"No," Taylor replied. "I've heard it's to attract the bugs so they can help with pollination."

"Attract a mate by smelling like death." Edward chuckled. "You might try that, sis."

Edward's joke was interrupted by a man screaming in pain.

Taylor ran back to the trail and the rest of the expedition. Grace and Edward followed. Taylor saw the men huddled around something on the edge of the trail. The screams continued and Taylor ran to them. He parted the gathering to see one man writhing on the ground in agony.

"What the hell…?" Taylor began.

"He fall to ground. Scream in pain," Abyasa explained.

Taylor watched the man convulse in pain. He held his neck tight. Taylor reached down and pulled the man's hands from his neck to see two small pinpricks.

"Get back!" Taylor exclaimed.

He pushed the men away from the man on the ground then looked upward. He drew his 1911 and fired. A snake painted in neon greens and yellows measuring more than four feet dropped to the jungle floor. Grace screamed. Taylor stepped forward and fired once more. The snake's head disintegrated into a cloud of scales and blood, tissue, and pulp.

"Temple viper," Taylor exclaimed.

Abyasa grabbed the man swaying on the ground in agony and translated. The man moaned something, and Abyasa stood and told Taylor, "He asks you end. Please to stop suffering."

Grace shook her head wildly in disbelief. She burst into tears and tried to say something but was pulled from the crowd by Edward.

Taylor waited until Grace was out of sight then put his pistol to the back of the man's head and pulled the trigger. The man fell forward in death and the men mumbled prayers in his name.

25.

"Temple vipers. They hang from the trees. Look like vines. They catch birds that way," Taylor explained to Grace and Edward. "They're lightning fast and extremely poisonous."

"But you shot that man," Grace wept. "You killed him."

Edward comforted his sister the best he could.

"I did him a favor," Taylor countered.

Grace started to argue the point, but Taylor signaled the conversation was over by walking away. He made his way down the trail to Abyasa, who was helping the men dig a grave just off the trail. The men looked at Taylor with both fear and reverence. They admired his earlier action but found it incredibly frightening that he could have pulled the trigger with such ease and almost no hesitation.

Taylor pulled Abyasa aside, away from the men.

"Tell them we'll pay his wife the money he would have earned," Taylor said, gesturing to the man being slowly lowered into the ground.

Abyasa nodded.

"I'll take them up the trail," Taylor continued, now referencing Grace and Edward. "Find a campsite. Take your time here then catch up when you can."

Abyasa nodded again then returned to the makeshift funeral.

Taylor returned to Grace and Edward and told them his plan. He said they'd leave immediately and find a place suitable for camp and that the others would follow. Edward nodded. Grace stared at him with eyes turned red from sobbing.

The three mounted their horses and Taylor led them away from the scene of the accident. They rode through the jungle for more than an hour without a word being spoken until they came to an opening Taylor thought would make for a suitable campsite. The clearing sat upon a small plateau that overlooked the valley Taylor planned to cross the next day.

Taylor dismounted and said, "Y'all can relax in the shade over there. I'm gonna scout around a bit. See if I come across anything special for dinner."

"I'll come along with you," Edward offered as he climbed down off his horse.

"I'm good," Taylor rebutted. "I'd rather you look after Grace. She's been through a lot today."

Grace wiped her swollen eyes and gave a nod of thanks to Taylor. Edward led his horse toward the tree line and Grace followed.

Taylor hobbled his horse, slung his double rifle over his shoulder, and made his way into the jungle. He traveled downward into thicker rainforest, watching each step to ensure his silence along the jungle floor. He came to the edge of a small ravine that opened into a large mineral lick.

"Lucky day," Taylor whispered to himself at the sight of a small sounder of boars utilizing the lick.

He counted eight animals. He picked the smallest which he estimated to weigh about 120 pounds and maneuvered atop the edge of the ravine until he had an unobstructed view of the animal. Something spooked the boar and they squealed and scrambled in every direction. Taylor raised his rifle and fired. He hit the boar just behind the shoulder and the force of the blast sent the pig cartwheeling backward. Taylor eased down the ravine to the downed animal. He cursed his shot for being too far back then forgave himself, citing the animal's running being the reason for his shot placement.

Taylor took a long pull on his flask then leaned his rifle against a tree and field-dressed the boar. He hoisted the gutted animal over his shoulder, grabbed his rifle, and began the hike back to camp. He arrived to find Abyasa and the men setting up camp. He gave the gutted boar to Abyasa and said, "See what the cook can do with that."

Abyasa nodded then told him that Grace had gone to her tent the minute it had been set up. Taylor nodded then asked about Edward. Abyasa said that Edward too had gone to his tent as soon as it was set up.

"Think they too hot," Abyasa offered.

"Maybe," Taylor agreed, not really caring one way or the other if that was the reason for their seclusion.

He made his way to his tent and showered. He had the men boil some water then waited for it to cool and used it to shave. He dressed and made his way to the dining fly where he sat in the shade with a cigar and tall glass of Arak Bali.

The afternoon came to an end and gave way to dusk. Edward and Grace joined Taylor for a meal of roasted boar but said little. They excused themselves after dinner, each saying that they were tired. Grace said that she was exhausted and went to bed. Taylor lit a cigar and went to his tent to find Grace waiting for him. She embraced Taylor and said how sorry she was, that she now understood why he had killed the laborer, and how she wished there was something she could do to help him erase the pain that moment must have caused him.

Taylor didn't respond.

He simply undressed her instead.

26.

"Setan?" Grace questioned on a trail of smoke.

She lifted her head off Taylor's shoulder and handed the cigarette to him. He took it and smoked.

"Setan, what?" Taylor countered.

"I might be pronouncing it wrong…"

"You said it right."

"What does it mean? That's what all the men said about the tiger. Does it mean omen? Because that's why those two left."

Taylor took another drag off the cigarette.

"Means devil. Or Satan."

"Did they really think that?"

"Don't know and don't care."

Grace lifted her head, stared into Taylor's eyes, and chuckled.

"Well, that's a fine attitude."

Taylor smirked and said, "Yeah. Well, it's mine."

A gunshot thundered through the air.

Then another.

Taylor tossed Grace's naked body off of him and onto the tent floor. He pulled on a pair of pants, grabbed his 1911 pistol, and ran to the source of the noise. Grace shook her head in startled disbelief then rushed to dress herself.

Another gunshot barked.

Taylor ran in bare feet to Edward's tent.

"Edward!" he yelled. "It's me. Coming in."

Taylor pulled open the front tent flap and entered to see Edward's back.

Edward was facing the open flap at the rear of his tent. His pistol was drawn and aimed forward.

"There's something out there!" Edward exclaimed. "Something huge."

Taylor eased around to the side of Edward. The man was ashen, sweating, scared to death of something. Taylor gently lowered Edward's hand then took the pistol from it.

"Tell me what happened," Taylor commanded in a low yet firm voice.

"There's something out there."

"Tell me what happened," Taylor commanded once more.

Edward suddenly snapped to.

He looked at Taylor for the first time since his arrival.

"What's going on?" Grace asked as she entered.

She was followed by Abyasa who entered the tent with her.

Edward turned and hugged Grace then pulled back and looked to Taylor.

"I was reading. In bed," Edward began. "I heard a heavy breathing. Groaning. I got up to investigate…" Edward paused to collect himself. He was still trembling and his voice was shaky.

"Continue," Taylor instructed.

"I opened the flap to see what was out there. It was a dark figure. Covered in hair. It roared at me. I shot," Edward offered before directly addressing Taylor. "It was an animal but stood on two legs."

"You sure?" Taylor asked.

"Positive. It had huge jaws. I hit it at least once…"

"You hit him?" Taylor questioned.

"Yes," Edward assured him. "My first shot. It yelled. Screamed. Something. I don't know how to describe the noise it made as I don't know what the hell it was."

"You shoot anyway?" Abyasa innocently asked. "You no know what is but you shoot?"

"Abyasa and I will go have a look," Taylor announced to Grace and Edward. "Y'all stay here."

Taylor grabbed the gas lantern hanging from the center support pole of the tent and led Abyasa into the darkness away from the tent.

"Go check on your men in case Mr. Beast Slayer in there accidentally shot one of them," Taylor assigned.

Abyasa nodded and left.

Taylor eased away from the tent and stepped into the jungle. He held the lantern in front of him with one hand and kept his pistol in the other. About eight feet from the tent, he partially tripped on something. He recovered and knelt down to see a large impression in the earth. It was a footprint of some kind but showed no real definition given the dryness of the earth. He stood and continued forward through deep ferns and knee-high grasses. A sudden noise caused him to stop. It was a low growl of some kind. Taylor raised his pistol and slinked forward toward the noise.

The growling got louder.

Deeper.

Taylor continued in on the source.

The growl was guttural.

Vile.

Taylor raised the lantern higher then jutted his pistol forward at the ready.

Taylor aimed and fired.

The thunder of his shot echoed throughout the camp.

Grace screamed from inside Edward's tent.

Taylor lowered his pistol and yelled, "Over here."

Abyasa was the first to arrive.

"He no kill no one," Abyasa reported. "All here. No bullet hole in anyone."

Edward and Grace arrived.

"There's your monster," Taylor said, holding a lantern high above something still unseen by Grace, Edward, and Abyasa.

Everyone gathered in the light to gaze upon the fallen beast.

The creature was black as coal with a crescent-shaped rust patch upon its chest.

"It's a bear," Edward exclaimed.

"Sun bear," Taylor added. "Big one too. I'd say maybe two hundred pounds."

"He too taste good," Abyasa said, licking his lips.

"You say he was on his hind legs?" Taylor asked, interrupting Abyasa's dreaming of food.

"Yes," Edward answered. "And he roared at me."

"I can see why you were frightened," Grace confessed.

"Must have stood around...damn near five foot tall," Taylor offered. "You got him with a pretty good lung shot. He was still breathing though."

"Thank you for taking care of that," Edward said.

"Are they dangerous? I mean...would they have killed one of us?" Grace stammered.

"This one won't be killing anything other than Abyasa's hunger pains," Taylor joked.

29.

Abyasa led Taylor and the rest of the expedition to the stolen tiger skins.

They arrived in the late afternoon when the jungle was baking in the heat.

Abyasa showed Taylor the skins, the tracks of the beast that had attacked them, and Arif's mangled body. The cadaver had rotted considerably in the days past and had been fed upon by a number of scavengers. The body only resembled a human in form, all other characteristics having been eaten, pulled away, torn, or sheared from the body. Grace was disgusted at the sight and left the scene and the smell to the men.

"It swing him to tree," Abyasa recounted. "Grab by leg and swing to tree. Back break."

Taylor kicked what was left of Arif over. Black flies swarmed from the body, carrying with them a cloud of stench and rot. Edward gagged at the sight and smell.

"His spine's broken. That's for sure," Taylor mused aloud.

"I tell you," Abyasa exclaimed.

"Yeah, you also said it was an eight-foot-tall orangutan that did it," Taylor countered.

"No orangutan!" Abyasa angrily corrected. "I say red ape. Red gorilla."

"No such thing," Taylor countered.

Abyasa pulled Jack by the shirt sleeve to one of the immense tracks.

"That orangutan?!" Abyasa exploded.

"I have no idea what that is," Taylor admitted.

For the first time, he actually thought there could be a kernel of truth to Abyasa's story.

Taylor knelt beside the track and traced the inside of it with his hand.

"You're right. Whatever it was, was huge," Taylor barely said aloud.

"Look these," Abyasa said, handing Taylor a few stray hairs. "It from monster."

Taylor stood and took the hairs into his hand. He studied them, made note of their length and color then smelled them.

"Orangutan," Taylor decreed.

"No orangutan," Abyasa barked. "Too short. Not right color. Like gorilla."

"Are there gorillas in Sumatra? Indonesia?" Edward asked.

"No," Taylor answered.

"Not gorilla," Abyasa exhausted explained. "It like gorilla. Much bigger. Walk on two legs. Beat chest."

Taylor looked around then to Abyasa.

"Whatever it was, it ain't here now, so I don't really care," Taylor expressed. "So, let's get my skins and make camp."

30.

Grace climbed off of Taylor and pushed her sweaty hair back. She rolled over, pulled a cigarette from the pack on the trunk at the edge of the small bed, and lit it. She handed the smoke to Taylor without partaking of it first, poured a tall glass of Arak Bali, and took a huge swig. She handed the glass to Taylor, took the cigarette from him, took a long drag on it, then eased down next to Taylor.

"I'll need your help tomorrow," Grace began. "To help me feel safe."

"You seem to take care of yourself pretty well," Taylor offered. "Thus far."

Grace shook her head.

"No. Not around Curtis. Around him, I feel like a child. He's scared me most of our relationship. I'm just worried he's gonna snap when I tell him it's over."

"It'll be fine," Taylor said.

Taylor wasn't really interested in Grace's concerns or what she had to say. He wanted her to leave so he could get some decent sleep. The last few nights she'd come to him in the evening, she had ended up staying the night and while she seemed to sleep fine, he found the arrangement anything but restful. Now she was talking about a man that Taylor was sure was already dead. In fact, Taylor wondered how Grace had yet to clue in on that fact. So far, they had suffered through stifling heat, been attacked by a tiger and a bear, had a man killed by a snake, and had laborers desert.

Despite all that they had witnessed and had befallen them, Taylor considered the expedition thus far to have been lucky.

The Barisan Mountains were an extremely dangerous place.

Uncharted and unexplored for the most part.

Taylor's train of thought continued through the trip and made its way to the tracks Abyasa had shown him only hours earlier. They were huge, resembled a human's foot, and were obviously left by something gigantic. Something apparently large enough and powerful enough to hoist a human from the ground and swing him around in a fit of rage and into a tree with enough force that it severed his spine.

An orangutan couldn't do that.

Not even an eight-foot-tall orangutan.

They weren't built that way.

And don't carry that type of ravage strength.

And if it had been an orangutan, he and Abyasa would have discovered the animal's handprints as well as its footprints, as the mostly tree dwellers used their hands in addition to their feet to walk on when on the jungle floor.

No.

An orangutan didn't kill Arif.

Something else had.

But what?

"Are you even listening to me?"

Taylor was brought back from his thoughts by Grace's question.

"Here I'm telling you how worried I am about tomorrow and you're not even listening to me," Grace complained.

"I've heard everything you said," Taylor lied.

"Really?! What was the last thing I said?"

Taylor didn't answer Grace's question.

He pulled her naked body to him and kissed her instead.

31.

Grace reluctantly identified her husband's remains through heavy sobs.

She kissed her hand then placed it upon the top of his head and whispered, "I love you."

Edward helped her stand and led her away from the body to her horse. She mounted the horse and followed a laborer named Ahmad back to the camp that was set a half hour's ride away from the massacre site.

"This is Robert Kreipe," Edward recounted to Taylor as he stood over the mangled body of what was once a man. "He was the professor's assistant."

Taylor nodded.

"There was a hunter with them," Edward continued. "Man named Andrew Matthes. I don't see him."

Taylor scanned the bleak desolation that was the camp and offered, "I doubt anything could have lived through this."

Edward agreed. He removed his hat, wiped the sweat from his brow, then asked, "What happened here?"

Taylor theorized that the camp had fallen prey to bandits or some remote tribe. That whoever attacked the camp took anything of value, killed everyone, and burned what was left upon their exit. Taylor continued that events such as this were only one example of the dangers of the region and one of the reasons he felt that the expedition he was leading was ill-advised from the start. Edward nodded in agreement and understanding then asked the beginnings of a question, "What should we—?"

"Unless Grace wants otherwise, we should burn the bodies."

Edward nodded then said that he felt he should return to camp to look after his sister. Taylor asked if he should wait to take care of the bodies or if perhaps Grace would want to have some sort of service. Edward replied that the bodies should be burned immediately and that they should return to civilization as soon as possible. Taylor said that he understood then sent Edward on his way.

Abyasa came to Taylor's side and handed him a small statue. The piece was carved from polished bone or ivory and stained red and black with some ancient dyes that had long since faded. The carving depicted a man or deity of some kind, and the base contained hieroglyphics of some language neither men had seen before. The figure's head was missing, as was one of its arms.

"This only thing not in thousand pieces," Abyasa explained.

Taylor looked at the bodies that lie in pieces, rotting in the sun, then offered, "All this for a little figure."

"That not all I show you," Abyasa said.

Abyasa led Taylor to a set of tracks in the earth.

"Same as attack me. Kill Arif," Abyasa explained.

Taylor studied the tracks then looked once more at the gruesome ruins of the camp. He guessed the tracks were almost a week if not older then convinced himself that the creature that had left them was long gone. He wasn't sure if whatever had left the tracks had wiped out the camp or had traveled through it after it was laid to waste. After seeing the tracks again, he wasn't sure of anything. Regardless, Taylor made the decision to leave before dawn the next morning and take a more direct, albeit more dangerous, route back to civilization. He wanted to get out of the mountains. He didn't think they were in any danger. He just didn't want to take the chance. And he wanted to leave.

Taylor told Abyasa to have the men collect wood, pile the bodies and any remnants of the camp upon it, and burn the lot until nothing but ash remained. Abyasa took his orders and gathered the men. Taylor mounted his horse and rode to camp, keeping his double rifle across his lap. He arrived to find Edward sitting under the dining fly smoking a cigarette.

"She'll be fine," Edward explained. "Still, I think it best we give her some time."

Taylor lit a cigar and poured himself a drink. He downed the drink without sitting and informed Edward that they would break camp and be on their way before dawn. He said that the men were burning the bodies and would return shortly.

"I crossed some fresh deer tracks on the way back to camp," Taylor added. "Gonna see if I can get some fresh meat for dinner."

"May I go with you?" Edward asked.

He saw the uncertainty in Taylor's eyes.

"Come on, certainly if I can drop a bear at 20 paces in the dark, I can drop a deer with a rifle in the daylight," Edward argued.

"You didn't drop that bear. You wounded it," Taylor reminded. "I had to put it out of its misery for you."

"It was pitch black."

Taylor smirked.

"You just said we're leaving tomorrow," Edward pointed out. "Let me take one nice memory, a trophy, from this place rather than memories of nothing but horror and death."

Taylor had reservations about leaving Grace alone but reminded himself that the cook was in camp, and that Abyasa and the boys would return soon. He reasoned with himself that what had happened to the professor's camp over a week ago had no real bearing on the rest of the afternoon and decided to indulge Edward.

"Saddle up then," Taylor offered.

The two rode back toward the site of the massacre then turned north and followed the tracks upon a narrow game trail. Taylor said the tracks were less than an hour old and that the deer seemed to be in no particular hurry. The trail narrowed still and ran up along a narrow ridge. Taylor and Edward dismounted their horses, tied them to a tree, and followed the tracks on foot. They had traveled almost half an hour when Taylor stopped dead in his tracks and knelt. He pulled Edward down and pointed to a wide area on the trail 30 yards before them to where a large sambar buck stood on hind legs, raking its antlers among the lower branches of a tree.

"What's he doing?" Edward whispered.

"Marking his territory," Taylor replied before instructing. "Take him just above and behind the front shoulder."

"While he's standing?"

"It doesn't matter. Just shoot him."

Edward nodded and raised the .375 H & H Mag rifle he'd borrowed from Taylor. He sighted in on the stag's shoulder, exhaled, and squeezed the trigger. The rifle thundered and the deer vaulted over at the shot. It spun around and tried to stand but fell over and out of sight.

"What the hell?" Taylor exclaimed.

He stood, made his double rifle at the ready, and had Edward follow him. They walked hurriedly down the trail to the spot where the deer was standing when shot.

"Son of a bitch!" Taylor complained.

Taylor and Edward both stood on the lip of the trail and looked down at the deer below. It had fallen off the path and into creek ravine that neither man had seen from his vantage point. Taylor estimated the drop at 15 to 16 feet.

"At least his antlers didn't break," Edward joked. "I still have a nice trophy.

"Yeah," Taylor concurred. "If we can get to it."

Taylor weighed their options then decided it would be easier to hike back to the horse and return on foot with rope rather than hike back and cut the trail so that they could bring the horses in to pull the deer out. Returning to the deer on foot would take time but not nearly as much as hacking a path through the jungle with machetes wide enough for the horses to travel. Taylor's only concern was that either option would have them back at camp after dark. He told Edward the plan and the two men returned down the path toward their horses.

32.

Abyasa led his men back to camp and immediately went about the business of making it both comfortable for Grace and Edward, and ready for an early departure. Abyasa had water boiled then cooled for Grace's shower, provided her with fresh towels and a drink, and took her laundry to be washed and ironed. He informed the men of their early departure for the morning following and had them ready the camp for a quick breakdown. Upon hearing a distant gunshot, he had the men prepare the fires in anticipation of Taylor and Edward returning with fresh meat for dinner.

Dusk came early to the camp thanks to the jungle canopy above that blocked all direct sunlight. The air came alive with the sounds of bats darting from their protection in search of food, the calls of insects and frogs, and the musings of small lizards and mammals upon the jungle floor. These sounds were quickly drowned out by the angry neighs and squeals of the horses.

Abyasa walked to the far end of camp to find all the men fighting to control the horses and donkeys. The animals bucked, reared, and pulled at the ropes that kept them tied to trees. Their calls of distress grew in frenzy, as did their violent actions. Abyasa screamed over the noise in query to what was happening but didn't finish his question.

A guttural roar tore from the rainforest. The air reverberated and carried with it the heavy weight of unease. The men looked to one another then stood paralyzed in fear as a red creature exploded from the jungle.

The monstrosity beat its chest, screaming in dominance and warning. It dropped to all fours and rampaged forward in an almost sideways gate. It collided into the first horse with the brunt of its shoulder and the animal collapsed when its ribs turned inward, piercing its lungs. The creature stood and grabbed a man in each of its enormous hands and smashed them together with such force that their heads were almost completely liquefied. The beast dropped the bodies and swung both arms into the next horse, sending it somersaulting into and on top of two men. The horse fought to stand but accomplished nothing other than grinding the broken bones in its legs against one another. The men pinned beneath the horse fought to push the struggling weight off of them. The red giant appeared over them and drove down clenched fists upon the horse's head. The equine screamed then fell silent when its jaw shattered. The creature drove down once more into the horse, crushing the men beneath it. The beast stood, beat its chest and roared, and tore at anything that moved or breathed.

Abyasa knew his only hope was a gun.

He ran from the storm of destruction toward Taylor's tent.

He saw Grace exit her tent and he screamed at her to run.

Grace saw the beast barreling down on Abyasa and screamed in horror.

The creature swung its arm into Abyasa and sent him flying across the camp toward Taylor's tent.

White blinding pain shot through Abyasa. His vision was blurry. He was dizzy. He crawled toward Taylor's tent.

He heard the creature roar.

He heard Grace scream.

Heard her sobbing. He crawled to Taylor's gun stand to the Tommy gun that leaned upon it. Abyasa willed himself to stand then screamed at the pain of his broken leg. He heard Grace scream once more. He grabbed the gun and forced himself outside the tent. He saw the creature towering over Grace.

He jacked a bullet into the chamber of the rifle.

Raised it to his shoulder.

Then collapsed in pain as his world went black.

33.

Grace was dressing when she heard the horses.

Their vocalizations were loud and chaotic, as were those of the men trying to quell them.

She thought maybe a storm was brewing and that perhaps the horses were responding to that.

Then she heard the roar.

It boomed through the camp with the force of thunder and for a moment, she thought it had actually shaken her tent. She heard the responses of horses and men, and the chaos and violence that echoed through camp. Men were screaming. Horses were neighing and snorting, donkeys braying and kicking.

Grace buttoned her shirt and stepped outside into the ever-growing darkness. She saw men and horses flying through the air, scrambling for safety, and the dark figure that towered above them all.

She heard Abyasa screaming then saw him running toward her.

He was screaming at her, something she couldn't understand.

Grace saw the gigantic monstrosity running after him.

The beast was enormous. It resembled a silverback gorilla but carried more human characteristics and was far bigger. It ran upright and seemed to be driven by some mission rather than blind rage.

The red ape swung into Abyasa and sent him flying through the air to the earth with such force that his leg nearly bent in half. Grace screamed at the sight then at the animal towering over her. The beast looked down at her and roared.

Grace screamed in response.

Watched as the ape studied her.

Looked her up and down.

Titled its head in wonderment.

Grace screamed and backed inside her tent.

The beast reached out and took her in his hand.

34.

Taylor and Edward were returning with the downed stag when they heard the shouts.

Then the roar.

Taylor kicked into his horse and drove the animal down the trail toward camp at a furious pace. Edward followed as best he could but the weight of the deer on his horse's back kept him at a fair distance behind Taylor. The men navigated the dark trail as best they could, driving their horses faster and faster toward the sounds of panic and fear. They entered the campsite to find it a place of ruin. The bodies of horses, donkeys, and men lay scattered and broken upon the ground, and the air smelled of death and fear.

Taylor saw Abyasa and dismounted. He knelt by his body then gasped in relief as Abyasa tried to speak.

"Abyasa," Taylor said in a calm voice. "What happened?"

"I screwed," Abyasa whispered. "Gonna die to be sure."

Taylor looked his broken friend and nemesis over.

"No. You're good. Not that bad at all," Taylor assured him.

"You call me by name. I die soon."

Taylor smirked at Abyasa's resilience.

"They're all dead," Edward stammered as he dropped next to Taylor. "And there's no sign of Grace. Where is she?"

"Abby," Taylor began again. "What the hell happened here?"

Abyasa did his best to describe what had transpired at camp.

He told Taylor and Edward of the red giant that came from the jungle and how it raged through everything and everyone. How it had crushed men or broken them in half, downed horses with a single blow, and killed or maimed everything within its path. Abyasa told how the monster had thrown him across camp and how his only thought was to get a gun so that he could stop the monster.

"Where's Grace?" Edward interrupted. "What happened to her?"

"It take her," Abyasa mumbled.

"Killed her?" Edward questioned.

"No. It to take. Carry her away."

Taylor stood. He took the Tommy gun from the ground, slung it over his back, and walked to his horse.

"Edward, get Abyasa on your horse and lead him down the mountain," Taylor commanded. "I'll catch up with you."

"Where are you...what are you...?" Edward blustered.

"I'm going after Grace."

"I'm coming with you," Edward insisted.

Taylor mounted his horse and spun it around then leaned into a stare at Edward.

"No! I said you're gonna take Abyasa down the trail. Do it now."

"But it's dark," Edward exclaimed.

Taylor spurred the horse forward and yelled behind him, "Then I'll find her and kill that son of a bitch in the dark!"

35.

Taylor followed the trail cut by the beast.

The creature had headed west out of camp and along a narrow game trail that led deeper into the mountains.

Taylor drove his horse forward at a constant pace stopping only to study tracks in the dark. He found strands of Grace's hair during one of these stops and an earring during another. These finds along with the absence of blood led him to believe she was still alive. He continued forward, keeping this thought in the front of his mind.

The trail narrowed then ended at the base of a tall jumble of rocks the horse couldn't follow. Taylor dismounted and tied his horse to a boulder. He took a long pull on his flask then slung the Tommy gun over his back. He grabbed his double rifle and began the climb upward and over the rocks. The rocks were steep, and the only light was that from the full moon above. He climbed upward for several minutes until the rocks gave way to a small ledge. The wall of the narrow shelf was covered in roots older than time, worn thin from rain and erosion. The ledge itself gave way to the view of a deep pool in a river some 20 or 30 feet below him. Taylor saw the muddy handprints left by the beast on the roots and knew that he had to climb the wall if he was to stay on the trail of Grace's captor.

He resituated the double rifle over his back and wrapped his hands around a narrow root. He pulled himself up and searched the wall with his feet for some sort of purchase. He found a rock jutting from the wall and used it to push himself upward. He climbed higher and higher in this manner until the wall gave way to a heavily wooded plateau. He scrambled out from beneath the tangle of roots that knotted over the edge and unslung his double rifle again.

The land before him was full of deep ferns bathed in moonlight. Large trees dotted the opening and the air smelled of musk and ammonia. Taylor found the beast's footprints and followed them. The tracks were taking him in the direction of an enormous dipterocarp tree. Taylor held his rifle at the ready and continued forward.

Grace was leaning against the animal that was in turn leaning against the tree in slumber. The area was ringed with uprooted ferns and brush stacked about in a manner that reminded Taylor of a nest. The creature snorted in its sleep and it subconsciously tightened its grip on Grace's mane of blonde hair. Grace saw Taylor in the moonlight and frantically shook her head from side to side in protest to his moving forward. Taylor silently shushed her with a finger at his lips and stepped forward with his rifle trained just above Grace's head, dead center of the beast's chest. Grace shook her head and tears ran down her cheek. She was scared to death.

And even more scared of what the cost of his not understanding her could bring.

Taylor silently shushed her once more.

The beast opened its eyes and trained them on Taylor. The beast roared and stood, letting go of Grace in the process.

Grace screamed, "No!" and Taylor fired his first barrel.

The 500-grain bullet slammed into the animal's chest with 5,140 pounds of force, pushed through its right lung, and exploded outward from its shoulder blade in a spray of blood and bone. The beast howled in pain and stumbled back. It grabbed its shoulder in pain then stared at Taylor with raging greenish-brown eyes. Taylor saw thought in the beast's eyes, and it frightened him unlike anything that had every frightened him before. The beast roared and exploded forward at Taylor.

Grace yelled once more, "No!" and Taylor put his second shot into the creature's right leg. The beast fell forward and lunged outward for Taylor. Taylor reloaded and walked toward the flailing beast.

Grace got in between Taylor and the monster, screaming over the howling of the beast, "Don't! We've got to go!"

Taylor pushed Grace aside just as she unleashed, "There's more than one!"

Taylor's eyes went wide at the realization of what Grace had just said.

The clearing thundered with the howls and screams of beasts.

The creature before Taylor answered with a cry of pain and fear. It stood on shaky legs and reached out for Taylor.

Taylor fired on the quick and the animal's finger flew off its hand in a storm of blood and shredded muscle. The giant ape arched back in pain and Taylor shot it between the eyes. The creature vaulted backward in death and Taylor tossed his rifle aside. He reached around and pulled forth the Tommy gun, preparing for the worst.

Grace grabbed his hand and screamed, "Come on!"

Taylor looked past the tree to see five apes of various sizes barreling toward him. He dropped Grace's hand, raised his rifle, and strafed the onslaught. The first ape caught the brunt of the 50-round drum and rolled forward in a bloody heap. Taylor continued firing and the night sky blazed in flames of red and orange and the sounds of clapping thunder. He fired until the rifle ran empty then tossed his gun aside and took Grace's hand into his once more. The two raced toward the ledge where Taylor climbed up.

The apes ran after them, their screams and howls piercing the night sky.

Taylor and Grace reached the drop off of the plateau.

The horde barreled down on them.

The lead ape was gigantic, a monster that towered over all the others. It screamed in fury and tore over the earth with a tenacity born in hell.

"We've gotta jump," Taylor exclaimed.

Grace looked at the river far below in shock and disbelief.

"No. I can't…"

Taylor grabbed Grace by the arm and jumped.

The lead beast skidded to a stop upon the ledge and swung down at Taylor and Grace in an effort to grab them. The beast's fingertips grazed the top of Taylor's head and the force of the slight action spun him away from Grace. The creature stared down at its escaping prey and roared in anger, beating its chest in threat.

Taylor and Grace shot into the water with the force of a cannon. Both plunged to the depths then frantically fought to reach the surface and the air it provided. They burst into the coming of dawn and sucked in air, fighting to calm their screaming lungs. Taylor looked up to see the creature screaming down at them in rage then felt the sudden pull of the current. He spun around to see Grace already some 15 feet downriver from him struggling in the pull of the river.

He swam toward her and together they fought to make it to the far shore, but the pull was too great. They river grew faster and stronger, tightening its grip on them. Taylor and Grace held hands as they struggled to stay afloat above the growing waves. Each gasped for breath and to keep their heads above the churning water. Taylor fought to keep facing downriver to see where the river was taking them. He watched as the banks grew in height, became steeper and steeper, then seemed to give way to nothing but sky.

"Deep breath!" Taylor screamed over the chop to Grace.

"What?"

Taylor and Grace plunged over the waterfall and crashed into the pool some twenty-five feet below. Taylor hit the rocks at the bottom of the churning pool and pushed off toward the surface. He grabbed Grace by the waist on the way up and they broke the surface together, both screaming for air. The crashing water from above them formed a whirlpool that pulled at them and willed them back down below the surface. Taylor fought the pull with all his might and together he and Grace swam from the pool into calmer waters. They swam down the river to the rocky shore where they crawled from the river on all fours. Taylor collapsed. Grace pulled herself on top of him and kissed him with the passion of a life renewed.

36.

"I just don't understand why you didn't put any shoes on," Taylor complained as he and Grace ambled over the loose rock of the river's shore.

It was now early morning and the sun was rising, bringing with it the heat and humidity of the rainforest. The air was filled with the smells of the jungle, the river that ran through it, and the sounds of buzzing insects and darting birds. Gibbons howled and shrieked in the distance, and sambar deer roared.

"Well, I don't understand why that thing took me!" Grace countered.

"Blonde hair and big boobs. What don't ya get?"

Grace stopped in her tracks.

"You are a vulgar, vulgar man. Have you no decency?"

"I had the decency to save you. You're welcome," Taylor chided. "Back to the shoes."

Grace huffed and continued forward on bare feet. Her hair and clothing were still wet and despite the growing heat, she felt a slight chill.

"I was getting dressed," Grace explained. "I heard the…the…whatever that thing was attacking—"

"It's not an orangutan," Taylor interrupted. "That's for sure. It's some kind of ape. But the proportions are off. Arms are too short. It stands and runs like a man."

"As I was saying," Grace barked. "I ran outside when I heard the men screaming and didn't give the idea of putting on shoes a second thought."

"We've moved on from shoes." Taylor smirked. "We're talking apes now."

Grace shook her head in disbelief at Taylor then continued following him the best she could.

They walked most of the morning, stopping only to eat found fruit or to allow Grace to rest her bare feet. They followed narrow game trails that dissected the thick rainforest and ventured beneath dark canopies and through sparse openings of grasses that stood baking in the sun. They paused to watch a herd of five elephants lumber through the forest and Grace stood in awe of their size and grandeur. Taylor only saw the lead bull and his ivory as a source of income, cursing himself for not having his rifle.

They continued walking well into the afternoon until Grace assured Taylor that her bare feet could take little more. He said he understood but continued pressing her forward. They had just passed through a narrow beam of light that shone through the canopy above when Taylor halted Grace. He held his finger to his lips in signal that she keep quiet and pulled his holstered 1911. Grace immediately panicked. She trembled at the unknown and at the remembrance of all that had led to this moment.

Taylor fired his pistol and Grace shrieked in horror.

"Hot damn! Would you look at that!" Taylor howled.

He ran forward and held aloft a dead mouse deer the size of a large housecat.

"Nailed him with a pistol shot at 40 yards!" Taylor bragged.

Grace sat on the jungle floor and shook.

"What? You don't like mouse deer for dinner?"

"I'm just…just a little frazzled."

Taylor dropped the deer and wiped the blood on his hands on his stiff trousers. He walked to Grace and knelt.

"That's understandable."

Grace nodded.

"Thank you," she almost whispered.

"Why don't ya rest over there by that tree," Taylor suggested, pointing to a massive hopea tree. "I'll get a fire going and we'll have some meat."

Grace nodded once more and again offered thanks.

Taylor left Grace and made a small fire then gutted the deer. He hung the small carcass from a low branch and constructed a small lean-to shelter utilizing fallen tree branches, vines, and large leaves from a dozen different trees. He pulled fern after fern and tossed them in a heap beneath the shelter then stamped them down until they were uniform in height.

"Is that our bed?" Grace asked as she walked toward the shelter for inspection.

"Bed. Floor. Six of one. Half a dozen of the other. Ya know how it goes."

Grace smiled.

"It'll do," Taylor assured her. "We should be able to catch up to Edward tomorrow."

Grace smiled again and said that she hoped as much.

Taylor stoked the fire then cut the deer into bite-sized pieces of meat. He pierced the meat with a long, narrow sapling and handed the utensil to Grace. She held the meat above the flame and turned it slowly. Taylor did the same with his meat and soon both ate and continued doing so until the deer meat was exhausted.

"That was good," Grace praised. "You did well."

Taylor nodded then complained about his lack of tobacco and alcohol. Grace laughed and said she wished she had a drink and a cigarette as well but that she could easily forgo smelling another one of Taylor's "rancid" cigars.

"Rancid?! Those are premium Sumatran smokes."

Grace rolled her eyes in laughter and tossed a small limb into the fire. The fire sparked and she watched the kicked-up embers float toward the canopy. Her eyes fell back down to the fire then glazed over in thought.

"I think he liked my hair," Grace suddenly mused.

"What?"

"The…thing…thing that took me. I think it liked my hair."

Taylor wasn't sure what to say. He thought for a moment to reaffirm to Grace that he believed the animal to be some type of ape then thought the better of it. Rather, he decided to sit and listen.

"It looked at me before it took me. Looked me up and down like it had never seen anything like me before. Like a child looks at something. I know that sounds crazy. Impossible."

"No. It doesn't. Apes are inquisitive animals."

"That's what you think those things were...are? Apes?"

"I think they're some kind of ape. But more, I dunno, evolved. They walk upright and, like you said, or implied, there's something behind those eyes."

Grace shook as a shiver traveled up her spine.

"I don't want to talk about it anymore."

"That's fine."

Taylor put another log on the fire and watched as Grace stared into the flames with glazed eyes once more. He tried to think of something to say or of something to offer that might make her feel better and safe but decided it best to let her deal with her trauma in her own way.

37.

It was early afternoon when Taylor and Grace spotted Edward leading a horse and an obviously pained Abyasa on a trail on the far side of a valley below them. Grace yelled for her brother, not comprehending the distance between them to be as great as it was, and Taylor fired his pistol in the air twice to get their attention. Edward stopped the horse and waved into the air in the direction of the shot though he wasn't entirely sure of where it came from. Taylor and Grace rushed down the mountain and across the valley to meet them.

They arrived at dusk to find Edward attempting to cook rice over a small fire.

Edward embraced his sister and Taylor took his .375 H & H Mag from its scabbard on the horse, looking to Abyasa.

"Can he travel?" Taylor asked Edward.

Edward pulled away from his sister and looked to Abyasa who lie under a small tarp shelter set up not far from the fire.

"He's been in an extreme amount of pain," Edward answered. "It took three attempts to set his leg."

Grace grimaced at the thought.

"His ribs are cracked," Edward continued. "His collar bone's shattered."

"Can he or not?" Taylor interrupted.

"No. Not if you want him to live. He needs medical care and lots of rest."

Taylor nodded in agreement then explained that they'd break camp as soon as Abyasa awoke. Grace and Edward agreed and sat next to the fire, each taking a bowl of rice. Grace told of the massacre at the camp and of the horrors of her capture. She told how Taylor had rescued her and how there were more of the creatures that attacked her still left alive.

Edward listened in wild disbelief to Grace's story then shared how he had shot a sambar deer and returned to camp to find it destroyed. He told how he feared his sister was dead and how he had strongly opposed not accompanying Taylor on his rescue mission.

Taylor let Edward and Grace speak alone and spent his time instead surveying what Edward had managed to salvage from camp. He hadn't brought much other than Abyasa, some food items, his rifle and ammunition for it, their pistols, a tarp, and, fortunately for Grace, a pair of her boots. Edward had also managed to pack along a few of his and a few of his sister's personal items.

"Where's my tiger skins?!" Taylor cursed into the darkness. "Where's my goddamn tiger skins?"

Edward left his sister's side and walked to Taylor.

"There wasn't room," Edward explained. "And they're not exactly necessary to our survival."

"Maybe not necessary for survival but necessary for my livelihood, yes. They're worth a ton of money."

Edward reached into a bag as yet unexplored by Taylor and pulled out an unopened bottle of Arak Bali and a handful of cigars.

"I brought these though."

Taylor grabbed one of the cigars and lit it then chased it with a healthy amount of liquor.

"You bringing these saved your life," Taylor exclaimed.

Edward smiled and Taylor shot him a frown, stating, "No. I'm serious."

Grace finished her rice and collapsed into sleep. Edward stoked the fire and Taylor ensured that Abyasa was comfortable then leaned against a tree away from the fire with his rifle across his lap. He stood guard there all night, getting up from his vantage point only to further build the fire or to check on Abyasa or Grace.

He didn't check on Edward though.

He was still pissed at him about the tiger skins.

38.

Abyasa woke shortly before dawn in the midst of a coughing fit. He held his ribs in pain with each cough then spit a small amount of blood. Taylor assured Abyasa that he'd be fine and that he needed him to recover soon so they could return to camp to collect the tiger skins.

"Tiger skin what get me into this pain," Abyasa complained.

"Quit you're bitching, Abby," Taylor chided. "I'm doing the best I can."

"No call me Abby," Abyasa muttered in pain.

Grace and Edward rose, collected themselves, and made ready to leave. The sun had just cut the horizon when Taylor helped Abyasa climb upon the group's lone horse. Abyasa grimaced in pain at the movement then settled into the saddle the best he could. Taylor handed Abyasa the reins then watched his eyes go wide in terror.

Taylor turned to see the creature that had almost grabbed him during his rescue of Grace before barreling out of the jungle and toward him. The beast unleashed a roar that shook the earth and raged forward. Taylor slapped the horse on the hind flanks and yelled to Grace and Edward to run.

Taylor raised his .375 H & H Mag, and Abyasa summoned his strength and spurred the horse around to charge the creature.

"No!" Taylor screamed as the horse bucked and fought its command.

The horse leapt to between Taylor and the beast.

Taylor jumped to his side to get a clear shot at the creature.

The beast plowed into the horse and tossed it and Abyasa aside in a fit of rage.

The red giant rushed the fallen beast, took the horse's head in his right hand and twisted it until its neck until it snapped. The creature stared down at Abyasa struggling to free himself from beneath the dead equine and reached out to grab him. Abyasa pulled his knife and plunged it into the creature's hand. The giant pulled its hand back in pain and anger then drove both its fists down upon Abyasa's upper body, crushing him.

Taylor screamed, "You son of a bitch!" and fired.

The bullet slammed into the back of the creature's head and sent its ear exploding outward.

The beast howled and grabbed where its ear had been in pain. It spun around and zeroed in on Taylor then launched itself toward him.

Taylor jacked another round in his rifle and took aim on the creature's kneecap, thinking the best way to deal with the monster was to turn it stationary.

Edward took Taylor's half-second of thought as hesitation or shock at the loss of Abyasa and stepped in front of him. He raised his Smith & Wesson HE2 pistol and fired until his pistol was empty. The creature howled in pain and agony as bullet after bullet pierced its chest.

Taylor angrily stepped to the side of Edward and fired.

The 300-grain bullet slammed into the creature's knee with more than 4,000 pounds of energy. The beast collapsed forward and onto the earth, writhing in pain.

Edward reloaded his pistol and walked toward the beast with his pistol ready to fire.

The red ape launched itself forward, took Edward into his hand, and squeezed.

Edward managed to get a single shot off before he was crushed to death.

Grace screamed in the distance and Taylor put two more rifle shots into the creature's head as it tried to stand. Taylor dropped his empty rifle and drew his 1911. The creature arched its back and unleased a deafening roar then fell forward. Taylor jumped on the fallen creature's back and put three quick shots into the back of the animal's head. The creature spasmed then fell still.

Grace ran to what was left of her brother and wept.

Taylor walked to Abyasa then cursed him and the world for him having passed. He walked to Grace's side, lifted her from her brother's side, and said, "Come on."

39.

The top of the crocodile's head exploded, sending shards of bone and scale, blood and brain matter flying in every direction. The remnants of the prehistoric monster's brain rained down over the rocky riverbank and its body twisted, rolled, and contorted in the throes of death. Andrew went through the motions of jacking another round into his rifle then remembered he had no more ammunition and instead gently leaned his rifle against a tree. He took his makeshift crutches under his arms and struggled toward the still-rolling lizard. The going was slow given his broken leg, the quality of his crutches, and the rocky terrain, but he was in no hurry.

He had nowhere to go and no way to get there.

Not yet, anyway.

It had been almost two weeks since the attack by some unknown monster that had left him battered and broken. He had suffered a concussion, a broken leg, and a dislocated shoulder, all of which he had to tend to himself, as he was the only one left alive from the expedition. It had taken him days to recover enough to move more than 10 feet from where the beast had hurled him. The concussion and the pain of setting his shoulder and leg had sent him in and out of consciousness for almost two days. Crawling on the ground in order to reach a fallen limb to make a temporary crutch had taken him another half day. And when he did manage to become fairly mobile, all he had found was a camp rotting away. He had found his rifle intact but no extra ammunition. Everything that could have burned in the camp had burned. Aside from two or three canned goods, there was nothing left.

He had made a shelter downriver from the camp. His original idea was to make the more-than-two-week-on-foot journey back to civilization but gave that idea up after a day on the trail. His leg was simply too unstable and he too weak to make the trip. So, he instead established a base camp in which to rest and recover.

Andrew gutted and skinned the crocodile then slung its five-foot long carcass over his shoulder. He took up his crutches and hobbled back to camp. He cut the crocodile into thin strips and hung them on a wooden rack above the fire to smoke. The smoke-cured meat would be enough to last at least a week. After that, he'd pack his way back to civilization so that he could fully recover and resupply. Then he could return to the mountains to kill that bastard ape once and for all.

This idea was the only thing that kept him going.

40.

Lima lounged and smoked hash on his overstuffed couch. He looked to the men that stood guard around him then back to Taylor who stood before him.

"That's quite the story." Lima laughed on an exhale of smoke. "If you wrote it down, you'd probably have a best seller."

"It'd be non-fiction," Taylor claimed. "Every word I've told you is true."

"Of that I have no doubt." Lima chuckled. "Far be it for you to make up such an elaborate lie just to avoid paying me money owed."

"Okay. So that does sound like me but not this time."

Those of Lima's henchmen that understood English laughed and those that didn't followed their lead and did so as well. Lima himself laughed then took another hit of hash.

"The professor and his camp are dead. No one survived the attack. The only thing the expedition found were pieces of pottery and crap like that and it's all smashed. Destroyed. And Abyasa's dead."

"Killed by a gigantic ape."

"I dunno what the hell that thing was," Taylor admitted. "The last one I killed…"

"That's right," Lima exclaimed. "You killed more than one."

"Three that I know of," Taylor admitted. "The last one was a monster. Son of a bitch stood over 10 feet tall."

"But it wasn't a gorilla or an orangutan?"

"No. Something else. More ape than orangutan but also man-like."

"Man-like?"

"The way it stood… And its eyes. There was more than animal thoughts going on behind those eyes. There was some kind of intelligence."

"But you described them as monsters."

Taylor reached into his shirt pocket.

Lima's men leaned forward with guns ready.

"Relax," Taylor announced.

Lima lowered his hand in a motion that informed his men to do as Taylor said. The men did and Taylor pulled an object from his pocket, holding it aloft. He walked toward Lima and handed it to him.

"That's a tooth. A front canine I pried out of the creature's mouth."

Lima took the seven-inch object into his hand and studied it with great interest. "It's carved ivory. Not a tooth."

"Trust me," Taylor demanded. "It's a tooth."

Lima put the tooth aside and declared, "What am I to do with you? You owed me for entering my territory without paying or seeking permission and now you owe me for failing to bring me the professor or his find."

"I told you…"

"And you have no money to pay me back."

"About that…"

"Normally, I'd have your head…"

"Don't be rash, Lima."

"But I know you are too valuable. I will call on you soon enough, Jack Taylor. And you will pay your debts in full. Or I'll have plenty of other teeth to add to my new collection." Lima took a long draw off his hash. He held up the tooth Taylor gave him. "Your teeth."

Taylor started to speak but was cut off by Lima's closing remark.

"You may go now."

41.

Taylor awoke in the Hotel Continental in Palembang Harbor to the sight of Grace dressing. He looked at his wristwatch to see it was early then watched Grace as she adjusted her hose and garters.

"Going someplace fancy this early?" Taylor asked as he leaned to the bedside table for a cigarette.

"Going home," Grace replied.

"Home? Like home, home? Houston?"

"Always the smart one."

"And you were just gonna sneak out of here while I was asleep?"

"That was the plan."

Taylor felt like he'd been punched in the gut and he hated himself for it.

Hated what he was feeling.

He felt rejection, pain, hurt, and sadness.

Grace had come to his tent all those nights. He had saved her life multiple times. And now she was leaving as if nothing had happened between them?

He jumped out of bed and pulled his pants on over his naked form. He rushed to Grace and said, "Explain this to me. What do you mean you're leaving?"

"Just that," Grace said as she finished buttoning her blouse.

"I... I don't understand."

Grace walked from Taylor to her purse and pulled out her silver cigarette case. She took a cigarette and lit it. She enjoyed two quick draws them turned to Taylor.

"Must I explain, Taylor? Really?"

"Yes."

"I didn't love Curtis and he certainly never hit me..."

"What?"

"And he didn't have any money. He had my money! And he was willing to throw it all away on science. On idiotic adventures such as the one that brought me here. I needed you to believe what I told you in order to help me get rid of him."

Grace paused for another drag off her cigarette.

"Ya know, I think you might have even killed him for me if I'd asked."

Taylor gritted his teeth in anger.

He'd been used.

"Don't look so hurt, Taylor. We had fun."

"The whole time? You've used me since the start," Taylor spit. "I risked my life to save you. And for what?"

Grace smiled.

"Blonde hair and big boobs. I think that's how you put it. You risked your life for blonde hair and big boobs."

42.

Taylor entered the small shop in downtown Acek and made his way past shelf after shelf of artifacts and primitive art to the back counter where he was met by Jeff Hammond.

"Taylor!" Jeff exclaimed. "Always good to see you."

Taylor held out his hand.

"Good to see you too, Jeff."

"Let's see what you have. I'm very excited."

Taylor placed the secured object on the counter and Jeff took it in his hands. He unwrapped the canvas cloth to reveal the statue Taylor had brought from the professor's destroyed camp.

Jeff ran his hands over the figure in awe.

"Exquisite. Very old. Centuries old. Neolithic. Painted ivory. Hand carved, of course, but with what tools?"

Jeff looked to Taylor.

"And you don't have the head or the arm?"

Taylor shook his head that he didn't.

"Shame."

Taylor agreed.

"I guess it depicted some sort of animal or God."

"Or both," Taylor added.

"Yes, many around here still believe in such things. Animal deities and the such."

Taylor nodded then asked, "What about the writing on the base? Is it writing? Can you read it? I've never seen anything like it."

Jeff held up his finger in the "wait" position then called to the back of the store.

"Kaliappa."

An old Sumatran soon appeared, his head and beard snow white against his dark skin.

Jeff introduced Kaliappa to Taylor then asked the man about the markings on the ancient figure.

Kaliappa took the statue in his hands and held it to the light and squinted.

"Very old," Kaliappa declared in an elder voice. "Very, very old."

"Can you read it?" Taylor asked. "Does it say anything?"

"It very old way of writing. Very old."

"Then what does it say?"

"It say… 'Behold'…No. That not right."

Taylor and Jeff watched as the man strained in thought.

"It say, 'Beware… Beware of the Kingdom of the Red Giants.'"

"Are you sure?" Jeff asked.

"He's sure," Taylor said. "That's what it says."

Kaliappa repeated the etched words, "Beware of the Kingdom of the Red Giants. It's a warning. Beware of the Kingdom of the Red Giants."

THE END

ABOUT THE AUTHOR

"If you mixed Ernest Hemingway, Robert Ruark, Hunter S. Thompson, and four shots of tequila in a blender, a 'Gayne Young' is what you'd call the drink!"
– Author Doug Howlett

Gayne C. Young is the former Editor-in-Chief of North American Hunter and North American Fisherman - both part of CBS Sports -and a columnist for and feature contributor to Sporting Classics magazine. His work has appeared in magazines such as Outdoor Life, Petersen's Hunting, Texas Sporting Journal, Sports Afield, Gray's Sporting Journal, Under Wild Skies, Hunter's Horn, Spearfishing, and many others. He is the author of Bug Hunt, Teddy Roosevelt: Sasquatch Hunter, Vikings: The Bigfoot Saga, Bigfoot, The Boggy Creek Narratives, And Monkeys Threw Crap At Me: Adventures In Hunting, Fishing, And Writing, and numerous other titles. His screenplay, Eaters Of Men was optioned in 2010 by the Academy Award winning production company of Kopelson Entertainment.

In January 2011, Gayne C. Young became the first American outdoor writer to interview Russian Prime Minister, and former Russian President, Vladimir Putin.

Check out other great
Cryptid Novels!

Hunter Shea

THE DOVER DEMON

The Dover Demon is real...and it has returned. In 1977, Sa
Brogna and his friends came upon a terrifying, alien creatu
on a deserted country road. What they witnessed was s
bizarre, so chilling, they swore their silence. But their lives we
changed forever. Decades later, the town of Dover has bee
hit by a massive blizzard. Sam's son, Nicky, is drawn to searc
for the infamous cryptid, only to disappear into the bowels
a secret underground lair. The Dover Demon is far deadli
than anyone could have believed. And there are many of the
Can Sam and his reunited friends rescue Nicky and battle
race of creatures so powerful, so sinister, that history itself ha
been shaped by their secretive presence? "THE DOVE
DEMON is Shea's most delightful and insidiously terrifyin
monster yet." – Shotgun Logic Reviews "An excellent horr
novel and a strong standout in the UFO and cryptid subgenre
–Hellnotes "Non-stop action awaits those brave enough
dive into the small town of Dover, and if you're lucky, you wor
see the Demon himself!" – The Scary Reviews PRAISE FO
SWAMP MONSTER MASSACRE "B-horror movie fans rejoic
Hunter Shea is here to bring you the ultimate tale of terror!
Horror Novel Reviews "A nonstop thrill ride! I couldn't put th
book down." – Cedar Hollow Horror Reviews

Armand Rosamilia

THE BEAST

The end of summer, 1986. With only a few days left until th
new school year, twins Jeremy and Jack Schaffer are on ver
different paths. Jeremy is the geek, playing Dungeons
Dragons with friends Kathleen and Randy, while Jack is th
jock, getting into trouble with his buddies. And then everythin
changes when neighbor Mister Higgins is killed by a wil
animal in his yard. Was it a bear? There's something big lurkin
in the woods behind their New Jersey home. Will the polic
be able to solve the murder before more Middletown resident
are ripped apart?

Check out other great

Cryptid Novels!

Hunter Shea
LOCH NESS REVENGE

Deep in the murky waters of Loch Ness, the creature known as Nessie has returned. Twins Natalie and Austin McQueen watched in horror as their parents were devoured by the world's most infamous lake monster. Two decades later, it's their turn to hunt the legend. But what lurks in the Loch is not what they expected. Nessie is devouring everything in and around the Loch, and it's not alone. Hell has come to the Scottish Highlands. In a fierce battle between man and monster, the world may never be the same. Praise for THEY RISE : "Outrageous, balls to the wall...made me yearn for 3D glasses and a tub of popcorn, extra butter!" – The Eyes of Madness "A fast-paced, gore-heavy splatter fest of sharksploitation." The Werd "A rocket paced horror story. I enjoyed the hell out of this book." Shotgun Logic Reviews

C.G. Mosley
BAKER COUNTY BIGFOOT CHRONICLE

Marie Bledsoe only wants her missing brother Kurt back. She'll stop at nothing to make it happen and, with the help of Kurt's friend Tony, along with Sheriff Ray Cochran, Marie embarks on a terrifying journey deep into the belly of the mysterious Walker Laboratory to find him. However, what she and her companions find lurking in the laboratory basement is beyond comprehension. There are cryptids from the forest being held captive there and something...else. Enjoy this suspenseful tale from the mind of C.G. Mosley, author of Wood Ape. Welcome back to Baker County, a place where monsters do lurk in the night!